SHADOWS OF VENGEANCE

BOOK THREE

THE ETHAN REEVES WEREWOLF DETECTIVE SERIES
BOOK THREE

RAE STONEHOUSE

LIVE FOR EXCELLENCE PRODUCTIONS

PROLOGUE: ECHOES OF VENGEANCE

The town of Daybridge was a place where time seemed to have stopped, its cobblestone streets and ancient buildings whispering tales of a history steeped in both grandeur and sorrow. But beneath the quaint exterior, a darkness lingered – a legacy of blood and fire that had never truly been extinguished.

On a night where the moon was hidden behind thick clouds, the air felt heavy with the weight of forgotten sins. In the heart of Daybridge, the old town square – once the site of the infamous Witch Trials of 1692 – stood eerily silent. At its center loomed a single, gnarled oak tree, its branches twisted like the fingers of the damned who had met their end there.

A figure moved silently through the square, their steps echoing the dread-filled marches of those long-past condemned souls. They paused at the oak, kneeling to brush gnarled fingers against bark that had seen countless horrors. Here, Mary Blackwood had screamed her innocence until the flames consumed her, clutching her infant daughter even as the smoke choked them both. There, Elizabeth Thorne, the midwife who had delivered half the town's children, had cursed her accusers with her dying breath, promising that their bloodlines would wither like autumn leaves.

From within the folds of their cloak, they produced the Bloodline Archive, its leather binding crafted from the skin of the executed, its pages stained with their blood. As it fell open, names blazed in crimson: Sarah Goodwin, hanged for healing the sick when the town's doctor had failed; Rebecca Clarke, drowned for speaking to her cats; Hannah Morton, burned for knowing too much of herbs and moon-lore.

The figure began to chant, their voices carrying the weight of centuries. The ground trembled as spectral forms materialized – women with proud, defiant faces and eyes burning with vengeance. Agnes Wheeler, whose prophecies had saved the town from plague, only to be rewarded with accusations of consorting with devils. Margaret Drake, whose only crime had been her beauty and her refusal to marry the magistrate's son.

The cloaked figure rose, revealing herself as Ravenna Blackwood, last descendant of Mary, the Witch Queen who had survived that terrible time. Her eyes gleamed with power as she addressed the gathered spirits. "Sisters," she called, "too long have we watched our murderers' descendants prosper while our own bloodlines were cut short. Tonight, we reclaim what was taken."

The spirits swirled around her, each bearing the marks of their execution. Katherine Mills, her neck still bearing the rope's kiss. The Preston sisters, their flesh forever scorched. Little Alice Gray, barely thirteen, when they accused her of bewitching the minister's horse.

"We shall visit upon them the terror they showed us," Ravenna declared. "Let them feel the weight of chains, the bite of rope, the lick of flames. Let them know what it means to be hunted, to be blamed, to be condemned without mercy."

The spirits dispersed into the night, each seeking the bloodlines of their tormentors. They carried with them three centuries of pain, of rage, of waiting in the dark. Ravenna watched them go, a cruel smile playing across her lips. In her hand, the Bloodline Archive pulsed with dark energy, each page a record of debts to be paid in full.

The revenge of the witches of Daybridge had begun, and no power in heaven or earth could stop what was to come. The descendants of the accusers would learn that some sins echo through centuries, and some vengeance cannot be denied.

So begins our tale, in fire and shadow, in blood and justice long delayed. The witches of Daybridge had returned, and their rage would shake the foundations of the world.

COPYRIGHT

First Edition

Published by Live For Excellence Productions

ISBN:

Ebook: 978-1-998591-34-3

Paperback: 978-1-998591-35-0

Audiobook: 978-1-998591-36-7

CHAPTER ONE

SHADOWS OF THE PAST

THE MORNING mist clung to the streets of Daybridge like a damp, suffocating shroud. Detective Ethan Reeves navigated the narrow alleyways, his footsteps echoing off the ancient cobblestones. The city had a pulse, a rhythm that he knew intimately over the years, but today, something felt different. A chill crawled up his spine, a whispered warning that the shadows held secrets best left undisturbed.

He arrived at the precinct, the old brick building looming before him like a sentinel of justice. Inside, the bullpen buzzed with activity, a hive of organized chaos. Ethan made his way to his desk, where his partner, Alice Chen, was already waiting, a steaming cup of coffee in hand.

"Morning, Ethan," she greeted, her eyes sharp and alert despite the early hour. "We've got a new case. Another disappearance, same as the others."

Ethan frowned, the weight of the unsolved cases heavy on his shoulders. Over the past month, a string of disappearances had rocked the city, leaving the police department scrambling for answers. The victims had nothing in common, no discernible pattern to their abductions, but Ethan couldn't shake the feeling that something sinister was at work.

He took the case file from Alice, flipping through the pages with a growing sense of unease. The latest victim, a young woman named Evelyn Walker, had vanished from her home during the night, leaving no trace behind. Like the others.

As they dug deeper into Evelyn's background, a startling discovery sent a chill down their spines. Ethan's eyes widened as he read the name on the old, yellow document. "Alice, look at this. Evelyn is a direct descendant of Abigail Walker, one of the women executed during the Daybridge Witch Trials."

Alice's brow furrowed. "That can't be a coincidence. Let's check the other victims' family histories."

Hours passed as they combed through dusty archives and online genealogical records. With each new piece of information, the pattern became clearer, and more disturbing. Every single victim was a descendant of a woman put to death during the infamous trials.

Ethan leaned back in his chair, his mind reeling. "What does this mean? Why target these specific people now, after all these years?"

"I might have an answer for you, detectives." A familiar voice drifted from the bullpen entrance. Lila Darkmagic stood there, her black trench coat a stark contrast to the fluorescent lights. "But you're not going to like it."

Ethan and Alice exchanged a wary glance. Lila had been an enigmatic figure in their past cases, her knowledge of the arcane both helpful and unsettling.

"What do you know, Lila?" Alice asked, her tone careful but curious.

Lila stepped closer, her green eyes flickering with an unreadable emotion. "The victims are being taken for a ritual. An ancient rite of vengeance, to resurrect the spirits of the executed witches."

"How do you know this?" Ethan pressed, his instincts on high alert.

Lila hesitated, her gaze distant. "I've seen it before. In another time, another place. The signs are all there, if you know where to look."

Before they could question her further, Lila turned to leave. "I wish I could stay and help, but I have my own demons to confront. Just know that the danger is far greater than you realize. The ghosts of Daybridge's past are stirring, and they hunger for blood."

With those ominous words, she disappeared into the mist-shrouded streets, leaving Ethan and Alice with more questions than answers. They looked at each other, the weight of their newfound knowledge heavy in the air.

"We need to find out more about these witch trials," Ethan said, his voice low and determined. "And we need to do it fast. Before anyone else goes missing."

Alice nodded; her jaw set with resolve. "Agreed. Let's get to work."

As they dug into the dark history of Daybridge, neither could shake the feeling that they were on the cusp of something terrifying. The shadows of the past wanted to claim the present, and it would take all of their skills and courage to stop the coming storm.

Little did they know their greatest ally and darkest mystery had walked out the door, a haunted look in her eyes and a world of secrets on her shoulders.

～

CHAPTER TWO

THE WEIGHT OF KNOWLEDGE

NADIA MARSH'S study had become a fortress of books and ancient texts, their spines creating shadowy canyons across her desk and floor. The windows were lined with salt, and strings of rowan berries hung from the curtain rods – protective measures that would have seemed absurd to her just months ago. Now they were as essential as her morning coffee.

She pushed away from her desk, rubbing her eyes. The computer screen showed a half-finished article about local zoning ordinances – her cover story for the Daybridge Chronicle. The real work lay scattered around her: medieval grimoires, photographs from the Necropolis, and her own journals filled with increasingly disturbing observations.

"Cross-reference complete," her laptop chimed. She'd written a program to scan digitized archives for patterns matching the ritual symbols they'd found in the catacombs. Another sleepless night of coding, another tool in her arsenal against the darkness.

Her phone buzzed – Dean Matthews again, probably wondering why she'd missed another editorial meeting. The timestamp caught her eye: 6:47 PM. She'd lost another day to research.

"Just five more minutes," she muttered, reaching for a leather-bound volume she'd "borrowed" from the restricted section of the university library. The book's pages seemed to whisper as she turned them, revealing diagrams that made her eyes hurt if she looked too long.

A knock at her door made her jump. "It's open, Ethan," she called, recognizing the detective's distinctive pattern.

Instead of Ethan, Alice Chen stepped into the study. Her eyes widened at the chaos of papers and protective symbols.

"Nadia," Alice said softly, "when was the last time you left this room?"

"I had a class on..." Nadia frowned. "Tuesday?"

"It's Friday."

"Oh." Nadia looked down at her coffee mug, noting the rings it had left on her notes. "I'm close to something. The symbols we found in the Necropolis? They're not just for necromancy. They're part of something bigger."

She stood, moving to her evidence wall. Photos, newspaper clippings, and handwritten notes were connected by red string, creating a web of connections that had consumed an entire wall of her study.

"Look at this." She pointed to a series of symbols. "These appeared at the ritual site. But I found similar markings in accounts from 1892, 1963, and..." she shuffled through some papers, "here – 1736. Always in cycles of seventy-one years."

Alice moved closer, studying the pattern. "The Dark Summer. The Shadow Year. And..."

"The Hunger Moon Massacre," Nadia finished. "Three failed attempts to complete whatever ritual our necromancer was trying to finish. Each time, something stopped it. But the price was high."

She pulled out a leather journal, its pages brittle with age. "This belonged to Elizabeth Marsh – my great-great-grandmother. She was more than just a historian. She was a Chronicler."

"Like you," Alice said.

"Like me." Nadia ran her fingers over the journal's worn cover. "We're not just recording history. We're keeping watch. The Marsh family has documented Daybridge's supernatural events for generations. I always thought they were just stories, local legends to make history more interesting."

She laughed bitterly. "Now I know they were warnings. Every strange death, every unexplained phenomenon, every 'accident' that didn't quite add up – they're all connected. And it's building toward something."

Alice picked up one of the books from Nadia's desk. "You can't solve this alone."

"I'm not trying to solve it. I'm trying to understand it." Nadia moved to her computer, pulling up a map of Daybridge marked with dates and locations. "Knowledge is power, right? If we can understand the pattern, maybe we can stop it."

"At what cost?" Alice gestured to the empty coffee cups, the untouched bed in the corner, the takeout containers piling up. "You're burning yourself out."

Nadia sank back into her chair. "I was there, Alice. In the Necropolis. I saw what almost came through. If that ritual had succeeded..." She shuddered. "I can't sleep anyway. Every time I close my eyes, I see those shadows taking form."

Alice placed a gentle hand on her shoulder. "That's exactly why you need rest. Clear eyes see patterns better than exhausted ones."

"Just let me finish this section," Nadia said, reaching for another book. "I think I've found a connection between the ritual sites and the old town wards. If I can just—"

Alice firmly closed the book. "The archives will still be here tomorrow. Right now, you're coming with me. Ethan's waiting at the Moonlight Diner. Real food, real conversation, real people."

Nadia wanted to protest, but her stomach growled traitorously. "Fine. But bring the journal. Elizabeth's entries about the 1892 incident mention a diner on the same spot. Could be relevant."

As they left, Nadia glanced back at her evidence wall. The red strings seemed to pulse in the fading light, like veins carrying dark secrets through Daybridge's history. Her great-great-grandmother's words echoed in her mind: "To witness is to bear responsibility. To record is to arm the future."

"Coming?" Alice called from the hallway.

"Yeah." Nadia locked her door, adding a protective sigil she'd learned from Lila. "Just remembering something Elizabeth wrote: 'The darkness always returns, but so do those who stand against it.'"

They walked out into the evening air, where the setting sun painted Daybridge's streets in shades of amber and shadow. Somewhere in her bag, Elizabeth's journal waited with its centuries of warnings and wisdom. The weight of knowledge pressed down on Nadia's shoulders, but for the first time in weeks, she didn't feel alone in carrying it.

~

CHAPTER THREE

THE WITCH QUEEN'S VENGEANCE

IN THE HEART of the Necropolis, the Witch Queen stood before an ancient altar, her eyes glowing with malevolent power. The air around her crackled with dark energy, shadows writhing like living things at the edges of the unholy light.

"The time has come, my sisters," she intoned, her voice echoing through the cavernous space. "Too long have we suffered in silence; our vengeance denied by the cruel march of years. But no longer."

Spectral figures emerged from the darkness, their translucent forms flickering with the same vengeful fire that burned in the Witch Queen's gaze. They were the spirits of the executed witches, bound to this plane by the injustice of their deaths.

"The descendants of those who condemned us walk the streets of Daybridge, ignorant of the blood on their hands," the Witch Queen continued, her lips curling into a vicious sneer. "But they shall soon learn the price of their ancestors' sins."

She raised her hands, and the altar before her burst into sickly green flame. A blackened tome materialized amidst the fire, its ancient pages whispering dark secrets to the hateful dead.

"With each soul taken, our power grows," the Witch Queen declared, her skeletal fingers caressing the tome's scorched cover. "And when the final descendant breathes their last, we shall rise again, to claim the vengeance that is rightfully ours!"

The spirits howled their approval, their ghostly voices merging into a chorus of rage and pain. The Witch Queen basked in their fury, her own power swelling with each fresh wave of ethereal anguish.

"Prepare yourselves, my sisters," she commanded, her eyes blazing with the intensity of her dark purpose. "The hunt begins tonight. Let the streets of Daybridge run red with the blood of our enemies!"

As the spirits dissipated, fading back into the nether realm from whence they came, the Witch Queen turned her gaze toward the unsuspecting city. In her mind's eye, she could see the detectives scrambling to unravel the mystery, unaware that they were mere pawns in a game centuries in the making.

"Struggle all you like, little detectives," she whispered, a cruel smile playing across her withered lips. "Your efforts will only make my triumph all the sweeter. For in the end, the shadows of the past shall devour the present, and Daybridge will be mine once more!"

Her laughter echoed through the Necropolis, a chilling promise of the horrors yet to come. The Witch Queen had waited centuries for this moment, and nothing - not even the meddling of a werewolf detective and his partner - would stand in the way of her dark destiny.

The pieces were in motion, the game began. And in the twisted heart of the Witch Queen, the flames of vengeance burned ever brighter, eager to consume all who dared oppose her.

CHAPTER FOUR

FEDERAL OVERSIGHT

THE DAYBRIDGE PARANORMAL DEFENSE UNIT'S headquarters occupied the supposedly abandoned fire station on Maple Street. Behind its weathered brick exterior and "condemned building" notices, state-of-the-art security systems merged seamlessly with centuries-old protective wards. Captain John Dixon stood in the command center, watching live feeds from the building's perimeter as three black SUVs approached.

"They're here," Officer Rodriguez announced, adjusting the screens to hide their more supernatural monitoring systems. The normal police dispatch radio kicked in, covering the sound of their supernatural detection equipment.

Lila hurriedly closed the Bloodline Archive, sliding it into a hidden compartment disguised as an old filing cabinet. Alice quietly moved her arsenal of blessed weapons out of sight, though she kept her silver-loaded sidearm holstered at her hip.

The federal agents swept into the briefing room, their suits impeccable, their badges marking them as members of the Department of Supernatural Security (DSS). Their shoes clicked on floors inlaid with protection circles disguised as historical tile work.

"Your containment protocols are... unconventional," Agent Harrison stated, reviewing reports on recent incidents. His eyes lingered on the "vintage" equipment that actually housed their most advanced supernatural detection gear. "Particularly your integration of... local assets."

"They work for our town," Dixon replied, nodding to Ethan who stood in the corner, deliberately letting his eyes flash wolf-gold. The werewolf's PDU badge gleamed alongside his protective amulet. "We've managed for centuries."

Through the window, Dixon could see more DSS agents examining their "historical" iron gates, likely trying to decode the protective runes worked into the metalwork. Their scanning equipment would be getting interesting readings from the building's extensive supernatural defenses.

"Times are changing," Harrison countered, laying out a thick folder stamped with federal seals. "The Boston Incident proved we need standardized responses. Three hundred casualties because local authorities couldn't contain the situation. The DSS is implementing nationwide protocols-"

"Which ignores local dynamics," Dixon interrupted, pulling out their own incident reports. "Daybridge isn't Boston. Our community has its own protectors, its own methods." He spread out their success records - supernatural incidents resolved with zero civilian casualties over the past five years.

Agent Harrison's partner, a woman whose badge read "Agent Buckly," was studying their wall of monitors. "Your response times are impressive," she admitted, watching the real-time supernatural activity grid of Daybridge. "But your methods... a werewolf as lead investigator? Civilian witches accessing restricted materials? Hunters operating with official sanction?"

"Each community has its own supernatural ecosystem," Lila spoke up from her desk, where ancient texts sat alongside modern laptops. "Trying to standardize responses across different localities-"

"Is federal policy," Harrison cut in. "Executive Order 13666 clearly states-"

An alarm blared - one of their supernatural detection grids lighting up red. Dixon watched the federal agents reach for standard-issue weapons that would be useless against what their sensors were detecting.

"Perhaps a demonstration," Dixon suggested, nodding to his team. "You can observe our 'unconventional' methods in action."

Ethan was already shifting, his PDU tactical gear designed to accommodate the transformation. Alice checked her blessed ammunition while Lila pulled up historical data on similar incidents in the area.

"Standard containment protocols-" Harrison began.

"With all due respect," Dixon interrupted, watching his team move with practiced efficiency, "you can either help us do this our way, or stay here and file your reports. But in Daybridge, we stick to what works."

The federal agents watched as the PDU team deployed - a werewolf, a hunter, and a witch working in seamless coordination with regular officers. Their equipment blended modern tactical gear with ancient protective elements, their communications mixing police codes with supernatural terminology.

"This isn't regulation," Harrison muttered, but there was uncertainty in his voice as he watched the team's practiced response.

"No," Dixon agreed, monitoring the situation through their sophisticated command center. "It's effective. Welcome to Daybridge, Agents. You might learn something about why local solutions matter."

The incident timer was running, and Dixon knew his team would resolve the situation long before the federal response protocols could even be implemented. Sometimes the old ways, adapted for modern times, were still the best ways.

Through the window, he could see the sun setting over Daybridge, the town's hidden defenses activating for the night shift. Another evening of protecting their community their way, federal oversight or not.

CHAPTER FIVE

THE MORNING COMMUTE

Rebecca Martinez pulled up to Daybridge Coffee, her police scanner quietly crackling with coded PDU updates beneath the regular dispatch chatter. The fresh iron horseshoes now adorning the doorframe gleamed dully in the early morning light - professionally installed last night by Miller's Hardware, one of the PDU's approved contractors.

Inside, regulars sipped their morning brew from ceramic mugs painted with protective runes – "authentic colonial designs" according to the signage. Rebecca noticed how Mr. Peterson, the high school history teacher, traced the symbols with his finger between sips, just as the town's "Historical Society" had demonstrated at last week's "cultural preservation" meeting.

The barista, Tom Nixon, wore a silver pendant, trying to pass it off as fashion. But Rebecca recognized the maker's mark - Tom Nixon's daughter was becoming quite skilled at crafting protective jewelry that could pass as ordinary accessories.

"The usual?" Tom asked, already reaching for the rowan wood stirrers that had replaced plastic ones last week. His sleeve rode up, revealing the fresh protection tattoo all food service workers were "encouraged" to get - disguised as a trendy geometric design.

"Extra shot today," Rebecca replied, watching Mrs. Sullivan carefully sprinkling salt across her threshold across the street. The old woman had lost her grandson in what the papers called a "home invasion" last month. Everyone who attended the funeral had noticed the claw marks. "Rough night?"

Through the window, she saw Officer Hayes doing his morning patrol, his new uniform badge glinting with more than just police authority. The PDU had finally managed to integrate their protective measures into standard police equipment.

"Just being careful," Tom said quietly, his eyes darting to the new security cameras. Their casings were inscribed with tiny symbols that definitely weren't manufacturer's marks. The "security company" had been recommended by Captain Dixon himself.

The morning news played quietly on the café's TV, reporting another "gas leak" investigation on Maple Street. Rebecca recognized the PDU vehicles in the background, carefully positioned just out of clear camera view.

The coffee machine hissed, momentarily drowning out Mrs. Peterson telling her book club about the "historical renovation grant" she'd received for her new iron fence. The pamphlet she was showing them looked like standard historical preservation guidelines, but Rebecca knew it contained carefully coded protection instructions.

"Here you go," Tom said, handing over her coffee in one of the new to-go cups. The "eco-friendly" recycling symbols along the rim were actually a continuous protection circle. "Added some of our new 'artisanal sweetener' too." He winked, referring to the blessed honey the café had started stocking.

Rebecca's phone buzzed - a notification from the town's "Community Watch" app, marking another "suspicious activity" report. The icon showed a traditional neighborhood watch symbol, carefully modified to include ancient warning runes.

As she headed back to her car, Rebecca nodded to Father Michael blessing the new "decorative" iron gates at the elementary school. Parents were arriving for drop-off, many wearing the "locally crafted" jewelry that had become so popular lately.

Her police radio crackled again: "10-91-P on Oak Street." The new codes were becoming second nature - supernatural disturbance, possible poltergeist activity. She started her car, watching the morning routine of Daybridge continue its careful dance between normal and supernatural.

The sun climbed higher, glinting off the "historical weathervanes" that now crowned most buildings downtown - each one precisely aligned with the town's ley lines. Another day in Daybridge was beginning, where every mundane morning ritual now carried deeper meaning, and protection wore the mask of tradition.

The coffee in her cup was still hot, the protective runes on the sleeve pulsing faintly with power. Like everything else in Daybridge these days, even the simple act of getting morning coffee had become part of the town's intricate defensive web.

CHAPTER SIX

THE WITCH'S LEGACY

ETHAN SWIPED his badge at the PDU's hidden entrance beneath the old fire station. The control room blended modern surveillance screens with centuries-old protection circles. Alice was already there, cleaning her crossbow while reviewing satellite feeds.

"DSS is requesting our incident reports again," she said without looking up.

"They can keep requesting," Ethan replied, noting how the room's tech seamlessly incorporated ancient runes. Standard procedure in Daybridge, where old and new had learned to coexist.

"You're here early," Alice remarked, taking a sip from her coffee. "Find anything interesting?"

Ethan sighed, leaning back in his chair and rubbing his tired eyes. "I've been digging into the history of the Daybridge witches, trying to find any clues that might help us understand what's happening now."

He gestured to a stack of old newspapers, their pages brittle and yellowed with age. "Turns out, the witches were more than just a footnote in the city's history. They were a powerful coven, with ties to some of the most influential families in Daybridge."

Alice furrowed her brow, her eyes scanning the headlines. "But why would they turn against the city? What could have driven them to curse their own home?"

Ethan shook his head, his eyes distant. "I don't know, but I have a feeling it has something to do with this." He held up a faded, leather-bound tome, its cover embossed with strange symbols and runes. "I found a reference to a grimoire, a book of spells that the witches were said to have hidden before their deaths. It's called the Bloodline Archive, and according to legend, it contains spells that could grant the user control over the dead and the power to reshape reality itself."

Alice's eyes widened, her fingers tightening around her coffee cup. "If that book falls into the wrong hands..."

"It would be catastrophic," Ethan finished, his voice grim. "We need to find it before someone else does."

They spent the next few hours poring over the documents, searching for any clues that might lead them to the Bloodline Archive. The more they read, the more they realized just how deep the witches' influence ran in Daybridge. They had been more than just a coven - they had been a force to be reckoned with, with ties to the city's most powerful families and a reputation for wielding dark magic.

As the sun began to set over the city, Ethan and Alice walked the streets of Daybridge's oldest district, a labyrinth of narrow alleyways and crumbling brick buildings. The air was thick with the scent of decay and the weight of centuries, and Ethan couldn't shake the feeling that they were being watched.

They turned a corner and stood before a run-down old mansion, its windows boarded up and its walls covered in a thick layer of ivy. Alice checked the address against her notes, her eyes widening in recognition.

"This is it," she said, her voice hushed. "The old Blackwood estate. According to the records, this is where the witches were said to have hidden the Bloodline Archive before their deaths."

Ethan felt a chill run down his spine as he stared up at the old house, its shadowed windows seeming to stare back at him with malevolent intent. He knew that whatever secrets lay hidden within its walls, they would not be easily uncovered.

They made their way up the crumbling steps, the old wood creaking beneath their feet. The front door was locked, but Ethan made quick work of it with his lock picks, the tumblers clicking into place with a satisfying snap.

Inside, the house was a maze of dark, dusty hallways and abandoned rooms, the furniture covered in a thick layer of cobwebs and grime. They moved carefully, their flashlights cutting through the gloom as they searched for any sign of the Bloodline Archive.

As they climbed the stairs to the second floor, Ethan couldn't shake the feeling that they were being watched. The shadows seemed to twist and writhe in the corners of his vision, and he swore he could hear the faint whisper of ghostly voices on the edge of his hearing.

And then, in the heart of the old house, they found it - a hidden room, its walls lined with ancient bookshelves and its floor covered in a complex pattern of runes and symbols. In the center of the room stood a pedestal, and atop it, the Bloodline Archive, its cover seeming to pulse with an otherworldly energy.

Ethan and Alice approached the pedestal cautiously, their hearts pounding in their chests. They knew that the book held the key to stopping the curse that plagued Daybridge, but they also knew that its power was not to be trifled with.

As Ethan took the book, a sudden gust of icy wind tore through the room, extinguishing their flashlights and plunging them into darkness. The whispers grew louder, more insistent, and Ethan felt a terrible presence coalescing in the shadows behind them.

He spun around, his gun drawn, but it was too late. A figure emerged from the darkness, its form twisted and grotesque, its eyes burning with an unholy light. It was the spirit of the witches, the source of the curse that had haunted Daybridge for centuries.

"You dare to disturb our rest?" it hissed, its voice a terrible, rasping whisper. "You dare to seek the power of the Bloodline Archive?"

Ethan and Alice stood their ground, their weapons trained on the ghostly figure. They knew that they were the only ones who could stop the curse, the only ones who could save the city from the witches' vengeance.

"We won't let you destroy Daybridge," Ethan said, his voice steady despite the fear that gripped his heart. "We will stop you, no matter the cost."

The spirit laughed, a terrible, mocking sound that echoed through the abandoned house. The ancient leather Bloodline Archive was nowhere to be seen.

"You are too late, foolish mortals. The curse has already begun, and soon, all of Daybridge will feel the wrath of the witches."

With a final, terrible shriek, the spirit vanished, leaving Ethan and Alice alone in the darkness. They exchanged a look of grim determination, knowing that the true battle was only beginning.

As they made their way out of the old house and back into the streets of Daybridge, Ethan couldn't shake the feeling that they were walking into a trap. The witches had hidden the Bloodline Archive for a reason, and he had a feeling that they wouldn't let it go without a fight.

But he also knew that he and Alice were the only ones who could stop the curse, the only ones who could save the city from the darkness that threatened to engulf it. And so, with the Bloodline Archive in hand and a grim determination in their hearts, they set out to face whatever horrors the witches had in store for them, ready to fight to the bitter end to protect the city they called home.

CHAPTER SEVEN

THE WITCH QUEEN'S WRATH

IN THE DEPTHS of the Necropolis, the Witch Queen seethed with rage, her skeletal hands clenching and unclenching as she paced before the ancient altar. The spirits of her executed sisters swirled around her, their ghostly whispers urging her to action.

"They dare to seek the Bloodline Archive," she hissed, her voice dripping with venom. "The werewolf detective and his nosey companion think they can stop us, but they have no idea of the power they meddle with."

She turned to face the spectral forms, her eyes blazing with unholy fire. "We have waited centuries for our vengeance, my sisters. Centuries of watching our descendants suffer, of seeing the blood of our enemies flourish while our own line withered on the vine."

The spirits howled in agreement, their translucent forms flickering with the intensity of their anger. The Witch Queen drank in their fury, feeling it mingle with her own until the air crackled with dark energy.

"But now, at last, the time has come," she declared, her voice rising to a feverish pitch. "With each soul we claim, our power grows. And when the final descendant falls, we shall rise again, to take back what was stolen from us so long ago!"

She turned to the altar, where the blackened tome lay waiting. Its pages seemed to whisper dark secrets, promises of power beyond mortal ken. The Witch Queen ran a skeletal finger along its spine, savoring the rush of dark magic that surged through her at its touch.

"Let the detectives chase their tails," she sneered, her lips curling into a cruel smile. "They are nothing but pawns in a game they cannot hope to understand. For every move they make, we shall be two steps ahead, guiding them ever closer to their own destruction."

The spirits swirled faster, their ghostly forms blurring into a vortex of vengeful energy. The Witch Queen raised her arms, her voice rising to a chilling crescendo.

"Go forth, my sisters!" she commanded, her eyes blazing with malevolent glee. "Haunt their steps, poison their dreams, turn their own shadows against them! Let them taste the bitterness of despair, as we have for so long!"

As the spirits dispersed, fading into the ether to carry out their dark mission, the Witch Queen turned back to the altar. She picked up the Bloodline Archive, feeling its power thrumming through her desiccated flesh like a second heartbeat.

"Soon, my little detectives," she whispered, her words echoing through the Necropolis like a promise of damnation. "Soon, you shall know the true depths of our vengeance. And when your final screams echo through the streets of Daybridge, I shall be there to savor every delicious moment of your agony."

Her laughter rang out, a chilling sound that seemed to make the shadows tremble. The Witch Queen had waited centuries for this moment, and now, with the Bloodline Archive in her grasp and her enemies stumbling blindly into her web, she knew that nothing could stop her.

Daybridge would fall, and from its ashes, she would rise again, to claim her dark destiny at last. And woe betide any who dared stand in her way, for the Witch Queen's vengeance would be a terrible thing.

CHAPTER EIGHT

THE NEIGHBORHOOD WATCH

THE PETERSON's Victorian living room was packed well beyond its usual book club capacity. What the public Facebook group innocuously called a "Home Security Meeting" had drawn nearly every home-owner from Oak Street to Maple. Ethan leaned against the back wall, his enhanced senses picking up the layered scents of protection: sachets of herbs tucked into windowsills, silver-threaded curtains that sparkled faintly in the evening light, doors freshly painted with clear sealant mixed with blessed salt.

Alice stood beside him, pretending to check her phone while actually monitoring the PDU's supernatural activity grid. The gathering showed up as a gentle pulse of protective energy - exactly what they wanted. Nothing to attract federal attention, just another small-town neighborhood watch meeting.

Mrs. Peterson, wearing what appeared to be a tasteful vintage brooch that Ethan recognized as a powerful protective amulet, stood before her antique fireplace. The "restored" iron grate featured carefully worked runes disguised as colonial-era decorative patterns.

"Now, for those who've just joined us," she began, her voice carrying the authority of someone who'd been protecting Daybridge homes long before the PDU existed, "we're discussing proper maintenance of traditional colonial door hinges." She held up a heavy iron hinge, its subtle protective symbols looking like mere decorative flourishes to the untrained eye.

Her husband moved through the crowd, passing out what appeared to be historical preservation pamphlets. Ethan knew they were actually grimoire excerpts, carefully rewritten to look like architectural guidelines. "Notice the specific maintenance requirements," Mr. Peterson emphasized, pointing to what appeared to be rust prevention techniques but were actually blessing rituals.

Mrs. Sullivan raised her hand, still wearing black from her grandson's funeral. "The hardware store's prices for these 'historical' materials-"

"Remember," Mrs. Peterson interjected smoothly, "the historical society is offering grants for 'authentic renovations.' The paperwork's been... simplified." Her eyes met Ethan's briefly, acknowledging the PDU's work in creating legitimate channels for protective materials. The town council had members who understood exactly what was happening - some from families that had been guarding Daybridge since its founding.

In the kitchen, a group of younger homeowners clustered around Tom from the coffee shop, who was demonstrating how to "properly season" cast iron cookware - actually a lesson in creating protective implements that could pass as ordinary kitchenware. The scent of blessed oils mixed with more mundane cooking smells.

"The neighborhood watch app has some new features," Alice announced, holding up her phone to show the seemingly normal community alert system. The new icons contained subtle markers that helped residents report supernatural activity without raising outsider suspicion.

A young couple who'd just moved to Maple Street studied the "historical" door knocker being passed around. Ethan caught the wife's slight widening of eyes as she noticed the symbols - she'd grown up in Salem, he remembered. She'd understand.

"For those interested in more advanced historical preservation techniques," Mrs. Peterson continued, "we're offering weekly workshops." She gestured to a sign-up sheet that cleverly disguised a training schedule for more sophisticated protection methods. "The historical society is particularly interested in preserving authentic colonial-era night watchman practices."

Ethan's phone buzzed - a text from Captain Dixon: "DSS surveillance van two blocks over. Keep it looking normal."

Right on cue, Mrs. Peterson switched to displaying old photographs of Daybridge homes, pointing out "architectural features" that were actually century-old protective measures. The discussion shifted to seemingly mundane topics: motion-sensor lights (blessed silver filaments), security cameras (supernaturally attuned), neighborhood watch rotations (coordinated with lunar cycles).

"Don't forget to pick up your welcome packets," Mr. Peterson called out as people began to leave. The innocent-looking folders contained everything a Daybridge homeowner needed to know: protective measures disguised as historical preservation, emergency contacts hidden in a neighborhood directory, supernatural warning signs presented as "historic building maintenance issues."

As the crowd thinned, Ethan noticed Mrs. Peterson's teenage daughter showing her friends what looked like a social media post about "vintage home protection symbols" - actually teaching them basic warding sigils. The next generation learning to hide supernatural defense behind modern facades.

"Same time next week," Mrs. Peterson announced, "for our discussion of historically accurate garden design." Her knowing smile suggested they'd be covering much more than period-appropriate plantings.

Ethan lingered until the last guests left, watching them disperse into the darkening streets of Daybridge. Each carrying pamphlets that looked perfectly ordinary to outsiders but contained centuries of protective knowledge, updated for modern homes. The neighborhood watch was changing with the times, but its essential mission remained the same: keeping Daybridge safe, one carefully disguised protection at a time.

Through the window, he watched porch lights flicker on up and down the street - each one installed with blessed bulbs, each motion sensor attuned to more than just physical movement. Another layer in Daybridge's intricate defensive web, hidden in plain sight behind the facade of small-town community organization.

CHAPTER NINE
WHISPERS IN THE NIGHT

THE BELL'S Diner was a Daybridge institution, a cozy little spot where the coffee was always fresh, and the gossip was always flowing. Detective Ethan Reeves and his partner, Alice Chen, had stopped by for a late-night bite after a long day of pouring over old records and newspaper clippings related to the Daybridge Witch Trials.

As they slid into a worn leather booth, Ethan couldn't help but overhear the conversation between two elderly men seated at the counter. Their voices were low and urgent, their faces lined with concern.

"I'm telling you, Hank, it's just like it was back then," the first man said, his gnarled hands wrapped around a steaming mug of coffee. "People disappearing in the night, strange symbols showing up on doorways and windows. It's happening again."

Hank shook his head, his expression grim. "I thought we were done with all that, Earl. I thought the town had moved on."

Earl leaned in closer, his voice dropping to a whisper. "You can't move on from something like that, Hank. It's in the town's blood, in its very foundation. My grandpa used to tell stories about the things he saw, the things he had to do to keep the darkness at bay."

Hank's eyes widened. "You mean the protection symbols? The ones they used to carve into the doorways and windowsills?"

Earl nodded. "I've seen them popping up again, all over town. Folks are scared, Hank. They're scared and they're looking for anything to keep themselves safe."

Hank took a sip of his coffee, his hands trembling slightly. "I heard that the occult shop on Main Street has been doing brisk business lately. People buying all kinds of charms and wards and whatnot."

Earl chuckled darkly. "Can't say I blame them. If the stories are true, if the darkness really is coming back, they're gonna need all the help they can get."

Ethan and Alice exchanged a glance, their meals forgotten. They had come to Daybridge looking for answers about the recent disappearances, but it seemed that the town's dark history was more tangled than they had ever imagined.

As they listened to the two old men swap stories and speculation, Ethan couldn't shake the feeling that they were on the cusp of something big, something that would change Daybridge forever. He hoped that they could unravel the mystery before it was too late.

Alice leaned in close, her voice low and urgent. "We need to look into this, Ethan. If there's a connection between the disappearances and the witch trials, we need to find it."

Ethan nodded; his jaw clenched with determination. "Agreed. And I think our next step should be paying a visit to that occult shop on Main Street. If people are looking for protection, that's where they're going to go."

As they slid out of the booth and made their way toward the door, Ethan couldn't help but feel a sense of unease washing over him. The darkness that haunted Daybridge's past seemed to stir once more, and he knew that they were running out of time to stop it.

But as he glanced over at Alice, her face set with the same fierce determination he felt in his own heart, he knew that they would face whatever horrors lay ahead together. They were partners, after all, and there was nothing they couldn't handle if they had each other's backs.

With a final nod to the two old men at the counter, Ethan and Alice stepped out into the cool night air, ready to face whatever secrets Daybridge had in store for them.

CHAPTER TEN

WHISPERS FROM THE PAST

THE ARCHIVES SMELLED of dust and forgotten things. Nadia hadn't meant to fall asleep at her desk, surrounded by century-old newspapers and her great-great-grandmother's journals. But exhaustion had finally caught up with her, and the text had blurred into darkness.

Then the dreams came.

She was standing in Daybridge, but not her Daybridge. Gas lamps cast sickly halos through a thick fog, and horse-drawn carriages clattered over cobblestones. The year was 1892 – she knew this with the strange certainty that comes in dreams.

"You shouldn't be here, Miss Marsh."

Nadia turned to find a woman in Victorian dress, her face eerily familiar. Elizabeth Marsh – her ancestor – stood before her, holding a journal identical to the one on Nadia's desk.

"This isn't just a dream, is it?" Nadia asked.

"The Caligari Cataclysm left echoes," Elizabeth said, gesturing for Nadia to follow. "Some wounds in reality never fully heal. They bleed through time, calling to those who can see."

They walked through streets that shifted between past and present. Modern buildings flickered like ghosts over their historical foundations. The air tasted of copper and ozone.

"Watch," Elizabeth commanded, pointing to the old courthouse steps.

Seven figures in dark robes ascended the stairs, carrying objects that seemed to absorb the gaslight. Behind them, shadows moved wrong, stretching against the flow of natural light.

"The Septem Umbrae," Elizabeth's voice was tight with fear. "They thought they could control it. Just like your necromancer thought he could control death itself."

The scene changed. They stood in a circular chamber beneath the courthouse. The robed figures had arranged themselves around a pattern carved into the floor – the same symbols Nadia had photographed in the Necropolis.

"It's the same ritual," Nadia realized. "They tried it before."

"Three times," Elizabeth confirmed. "Each attempt weakened the barriers. Each failure left scars."

The air crackled with energy. The robed figures began to chant in a language that made Nadia's ears bleed. In the center of their circle, reality began to tear.

"Look closely," Elizabeth urged. "See what they couldn't."

Nadia forced herself to watch as the tear widened. Through it, she glimpsed something vast and ancient, a presence that defied comprehension. But at the circle's edge, nearly hidden by the shadows...

"The wards," she gasped. "There were protective wards already in place. Built into the foundation."

"By the founders," Elizabeth nodded. "The Septem Umbrae thought they were working with the town's power. They didn't realize they were working against its original purpose."

The scene dissolved into chaos. Screams echoed through time as the ritual collapsed, taking most of the chamber with it. But before the vision faded, Nadia saw Elizabeth rushing in with others – ancestors of faces she knew. They were carrying objects, forming their own circle...

Nadia jerked awake, her heart pounding. Papers had scattered across her desk, but Elizabeth's journal lay open before her, pages turning by themselves in a nonexistent wind.

Her phone showed 4:33 AM. With trembling fingers, she began to write:

"The Caligari Cataclysm wasn't just an event – it was an attempt. The ritual chamber beneath the old courthouse... the original wards... it's all connected. The town itself is a ward, designed to prevent exactly what they tried to do. What they're still trying to do..."

Her hand cramped, but she couldn't stop writing. The dream was already fading, but certain images remained sharp: the pattern on the floor, the objects the robed figures carried, the way the shadows moved.

A text message lit up her phone: "Can't sleep either? - Ethan"

She replied: "Need to show you something. Bring Alice. It's about the wards."

Standing, Nadia moved to her evidence wall. With shaking hands, she began rearranging the strings, creating a new pattern. When she stepped back, she saw it clearly for the first time – the shape of Daybridge's streets, the placement of its oldest buildings, the flow of its underground streams. All forming a vast protective circle, with the courthouse at its center.

"The founders knew," she whispered. "They built the town as a seal."

Her computer chimed. The pattern-recognition software had analyzed the courthouse blueprints. On her screen, overlaid on the modern building plans, she could see the remnants of that underground chamber.

Another text from Ethan: "On our way. You okay?"

She stared at the message, thinking of Elizabeth's face, of the terror and determination she'd seen there. Finally, she typed: "No. But I understand now. It was never about bringing something in. It's about keeping something out. And the barrier is weakening."

Outside her window, dawn was breaking over Daybridge. The morning light caught the protective crystals Nadia had hung there, casting prismatic shadows that, just for a moment, looked like figures in robes. Nadia shivered and drew the curtains.

She had work to do before Ethan and Alice arrived. The past had finally spoken clearly, and its warning couldn't wait.

∽

CHAPTER ELEVEN

A HAUNTING ALLIANCE

THE BLACK CAULDRON was a dingy little occult shop, tucked away in the labyrinthine streets of Daybridge's red-light district where the town's ley lines intersected in dangerous patterns. Its grimy windows, strategically clouded to hide the true nature of its inventory, and peeling paint concealed sophisticated supernatural security measures. PDU-approved protective sigils were hidden beneath layers of graffiti, while genuine magical artifacts sat camouflaged among tourist-trap trinkets.

Detective Ethan Reeves and his partner, Alice Chen, stood outside the shop's entrance, their faces grim as they studied the faded sigils and arcane symbols that adorned the heavy wooden door. Ethan's enhanced senses picked up the thrumming of old magic - protections far older than the building itself.

Alice adjusted her shoulder holster, checking both her standard-issue weapon and the blessed silver dagger concealed beneath her jacket. "Are you sure about this?" she asked, her voice tight with tension as she glanced over at Ethan. "Lila's not exactly known for her trustworthiness. The last time the PDU worked with her..."

"The Hartford incident," Ethan finished. "I remember." His hand unconsciously touched the scar on his side - a reminder of how complicated dealing with Daybridge's magical underground could be. "But right now, she's the only lead we've got. If anyone can help us decipher the ritual, it's her."

The crime scene photos in his pocket felt heavy - three victims, their bodies arranged in patterns that matched nothing in the PDU's official grimoire. But Lila's knowledge went deeper, darker, drawing from sources the official channels wouldn't touch.

With a deep breath, he pushed open the door and stepped inside. The musty scent of old books and dried herbs hit him like a physical blow, along with subtler magical traces his wolf senses could detect: powdered dragon bone, essence of midnight bloom, crystallized moonlight. The shop was dimly lit, the only illumination coming from a handful of flickering candles - each one, Ethan noted, placed at precise points to maintain a complex warding circle.

A crystal ball sat on a rickety table in the center of the room, its eerie glow pulsing in sync with the town's supernatural activity grid. Behind the counter, shelves held what appeared to be cheap tourist souvenirs mixed with genuine magical artifacts - an organization system only initiates could decode.

As his eyes adjusted to the gloom, Ethan saw movement in the shadows. Lila emerged like a creature of darkness taking form, her raven hair gleaming in the candlelight. Her emerald eyes glinted with a hint of mischief, but Ethan caught the calculating assessment behind her casual stance. She wore what appeared to be vintage bohemian fashion, but he recognized the protective symbols woven into the fabric, the rings on her fingers that held more power than simple jewelry.

"Well, well," she purred, her voice like honey and whiskey, carrying undertones of power that made Ethan's wolf instincts stir. "Look what the cat dragged in. The PDU's finest, darkening my humble doorway." She moved behind the counter, her fingers trailing over items that responded to her touch with subtle magical pulses. "Must be serious if you're willing to risk your superiors knowing you came here."

Alice stepped forward, producing the case file. "Three victims in two weeks. The ritual pattern-"

"Ah," Lila interrupted, her playful demeanor shifting to something sharper. She reached beneath the counter and pulled out an ancient tome, its binding made of materials Ethan preferred not to identify. "You're not the only ones who've noticed. The old patterns are changing, aren't they?"

She opened the book, revealing pages of forbidden knowledge that the PDU's official archives had long ago purged. "The question is," she continued, fixing them with a knowing stare, "how far are Daybridge's protectors willing to go to stop it? Some knowledge comes with a price."

Ethan moved closer, noting how the shadows in the shop's corners seemed to deepen. "Name it."

"Information exchange," Lila said, pulling out another book, this one bound in more conventional leather. "There are things happening in Daybridge that your official channels won't acknowledge. I help you with your ritual killer, you keep me informed about certain... developments."

"You know we can't-" Alice began.

"Then people will keep dying," Lila cut in smoothly. "The old powers are stirring, detectives. Your standard procedures won't be enough. Sometimes you need to dance with shadows to fight the dark."

Ethan caught Alice's eye, seeing his own conflict reflected there. They both knew turning to Lila was dangerous - she played by her own rules, walked the line between light and dark. But as another candle flickered, casting symbols on the wall that matched their crime scene photos, they also knew they were running out of options.

"Show us what you know," Ethan said finally. "But remember - you're under PDU observation. Step out of line-"

"Darling," Lila smiled, the candlelight making her look momentarily inhuman, "I never step out of line. I just redraw them when necessary."

She opened the ancient tome to a marked page. "Now, about your ritual killer - have you ever heard of the Midnight Court?"

The candles dimmed slightly as she began to speak, sharing forbidden knowledge that would change their investigation - and perhaps Daybridge itself - forever. In the shadows of the Black Cauldron, a dangerous alliance was forming, one that would test the boundaries between official authority and ancient power.

CHAPTER TWELVE

SHADOWS OF THE PAST

THE STREETS of Prague were a labyrinth of narrow alleys and ancient secrets, the perfect place for people who wished to remain unseen. Lila Darkmagic moved through the shadows like a wraith, her black cloak billowing behind her in the chilly night air.

She had come to this city seeking answers, hoping to undo the dark ritual she had performed all those years ago. The memory of that night still haunted her, the screams of the sacrifices echoing in her mind, the taste of blood and ashes on her tongue.

Lila paused before a crumbling stone archway, the entrance to a hidden courtyard that few knew existed. She could feel the dark energy emanating from within, a palpable force that set her teeth on edge and made her skin crawl.

With a steadying breath, she stepped through the archway, the air shimmering around her as she crossed the threshold. The courtyard was just as she remembered it, the stone walls covered in arcane symbols and the ground stained with the remnants of dark magic.

At the center of the courtyard stood a stone altar, its surface carved with the same twisted runes that had been etched into her memory all those years ago. Lila approached it slowly, her fingers trembling as she traced the ancient markings, the power within them thrumming through her veins like a siren's call.

She closed her eyes, the memories washing over her in a tidal wave of grief and regret. She saw herself, young and foolish, drunk on the promise of power and immortality. She saw the ritual, the blood and the fire, the innocent lives snuffed out like candles in the wind.

And she saw the moment it all went wrong, the moment when the darkness she had unleashed consumed her utterly. Lila had fled then, her heart shattered, and her soul stained with the guilt of what she had done.

Now, standing before the altar once more, Lila knew that she had to make things right. She had to break the bond that tied her to the dark magic; to undo the evil she had wrought upon the world.

But as she began to chant the ancient words of power, she could feel the darkness stirring around her, the whispers of the damned echoing in her mind. She knew that the road ahead would be long and treacherous, that the price of redemption would be higher than she ever could have imagined.

And yet, she would not turn back. She would face the shadows of her past, no matter the cost. For the sake of the innocent, for the sake of her own shattered soul, Lila Darkmagic would see this through to the bitter end.

～

CHAPTER THIRTEEN

THE PRICE OF KNOWLEDGE

THE NIGHTMARE always started the same way.

Nadia stood in her study, surrounded by her carefully organized research. But the red strings connecting her evidence began to pulse like living veins, and the photographs bled black ink that formed impossible symbols on her walls.

Tonight's vision felt different. More real.

Her reflection in the computer screen wasn't her own – it showed a woman with hollow eyes and gray-streaked hair, though Nadia was only thirty-four. As she watched, dark circles under her eyes deepened into bruise-like shadows that spread across her face.

"Knowledge demands its price," her reflection whispered, mouth moving wrong. "Are you prepared to pay it?"

Nadia jerked awake, knocking over a stack of ancient texts. Her neck cracked as she straightened – she'd fallen asleep at her desk again. The clock read 4:17 AM. Another night lost to research.

Her hands shook as she reached for her coffee mug, finding it empty. The tremors weren't just from caffeine anymore. Ever since she'd

41

started translating the Voynich manuscript passages about the Caligari Cataclysm, her body had been rebelling. Headaches that made her vision blur. Nosebleeds that left rust-colored stains on her notes. Dreams that followed her into waking hours.

"Just need to finish this section," she muttered, pulling the manuscript closer. The symbols seemed to crawl across the page, rearranging themselves when she wasn't looking directly at them. She'd learned to read them sideways, through her peripheral vision.

Her phone buzzed – another worried text from Alice:

"You missed dinner. Again. Please tell me you're sleeping."

Nadia ignored it, focusing on her translation notes:

"When the seventh seal breaks, the void between... no, that's wrong. The void beneath? Behind? The words keep shifting..."

A sharp pain lanced through her temple. Another nosebleed started, drops falling onto her notebook. The red spots spread and morphed into familiar symbols – the same ones from the Necropolis ritual.

"Not real," she whispered, pressing her sleeve against her nose. "It's not real."

But she knew better. The line between reality and nightmare had grown treacherously thin. Last week, she'd found her research notes written in her own blood, with no memory of writing them. Yesterday, she'd spent an hour talking to Elizabeth Marsh before realizing her ancestor had been dead for a century.

Her laptop chimed with an incoming video call. Ethan's face appeared on screen, concern evident even through the poor connection.

"Jesus, Nadia. You look like hell."

"Thanks," she managed a weak smile. "You should see the other guy."

"This isn't funny. Alice says you haven't been outside in days."

"I'm on sabbatical."

"You're obsessed." His voice softened. "We're worried about you."

"I'm fine." She angled the camera away from the wall where shadows were gathering in impossible shapes. "I'm close to something, Ethan. The manuscript, Elizabeth's journals, the ritual site photos – they're all pointing to something bigger."

"At what cost? When was the last time you actually slept? Ate something that wasn't coffee?"

She ignored the questions, shuffling through her papers. "Listen, I found references to a convergence. The ley lines are aligning like they did in 1892, but there's more. The barrier between worlds is thinning. What came through in the Necropolis was just the beginning."

"Nadia—"

"They're not just dreams anymore!" Her voice cracked. "I see things when I'm awake now. The knowledge... it wants to be found. It shows me things. Important things."

"It's killing you," Ethan said bluntly.

"Maybe that's the price." She looked down at her hands, noticing for the first time how thin her wrists had become, how her skin seemed almost translucent. "Elizabeth paid it. So did every Marsh before me. We're not just chroniclers, Ethan. We're witnesses. Guards."

The shadows behind her shifted again, taking forms that made Ethan's wolf stir uneasily. "I'm coming over."

"No!" She glanced nervously at the darkness. "I mean, not yet. I need to finish this first. The knowledge... it's volatile. Dangerous. I need to understand it before I can share it safely."

"There's nothing safe about what you're doing."

A book fell from her shelf, pages fluttering open to reveal diagrams that shouldn't have been there. Her nose started bleeding again.

"I have to go," she said quickly, reaching for the laptop.

"Nadia, wait—"

She slammed the computer shut, plunging the room into darkness. The shadows gathered closer, whispering in languages that hurt to hear. Her notes glowed faintly, symbols pulsing in time with her racing heart.

"Show me," she whispered to the darkness. "Show me what you need me to see."

The knowledge came, as it always did, in fragments that cut like broken glass. Images flooded her mind: the network of ley lines beneath Daybridge glowing like funeral pyres, the courthouse foundations cracking along symbolic fault lines, something vast and hungry pressing against the thinning walls of reality.

She wrote frantically, filling pages with warnings and revelations. Her hand cramped, but she couldn't stop. The knowledge demanded to be recorded, preserved, understood. Even as it drained her, changed her, consumed her.

Hours later, Alice found her unconscious at her desk, surrounded by papers covered in eldritch symbols and equations that seemed to move when viewed directly. As Alice tried

to stabilize her friend, she noticed Nadia's latest journal entry:

"The price of knowledge isn't just in learning it. It's in carrying it. Bearing it. Some truths are too heavy for one mind to hold. But someone has to. Someone has to see. Someone has to remember. Someone has to—"

The writing trailed off into a spiral of increasingly frantic symbols.

In her feverish sleep, Nadia smiled. She had seen. She had understood. And soon, she would tell them everything – if her mind survived the knowing.

~

CHAPTER FOURTEEN

INTERNATIONAL CONCERNS

THE PDU's secure conference room hummed with protective energy, advanced technology seamlessly blending with ancient wards. Multiple screens displayed faces from across the globe, while a holographic map in the center showed supernatural activity patterns spanning continents. Captain Dixon stood at the head of the table, flanked by his core team: Ethan, Alice, and Lila, whose presence as a civilian consultant had raised more than a few international eyebrows.

Representatives from various global agencies filled the screens: Commander Elizabeth Braithwaite from Britain's Supernatural Containment Division, her office in the Tower of London visible behind her; Director Tanaka of Japan's Yokai Response Unit, surrounded by screens showing real-time monitoring of Japan's spiritual barriers; and Dr. Klaus Weber from the EU's Paranormal Activity Monitoring Agency, his Swiss headquarters displaying a wall of ancient protective artifacts.

"The surge in supernatural activity isn't isolated to Daybridge," Commander Braithwaite explained, her crisp British accent carrying authority earned from decades of service. She shared data showing global hotspots, each pulsing with increasing intensity. "London's seen a 300% increase in metaphysical disturbances. The old wards beneath Westminster are straining."

"Tokyo's barrier system is reporting similar anomalies," Director Tanaka added, his hands moving over traditional ofuda papers even as he manipulated modern tracking systems. "Ancient yokai we haven't seen in centuries are becoming active again."

"But your town's readings are... unique," Dr. Weber interjected, zooming in on Daybridge's energy signature. "The patterns suggest a level of integration between supernatural and mundane that violates several international protocols."

"Our history runs deep," Lila interjected, the Bloodline Archive open before her, its pages shifting slightly in currents of magical energy only she could see. Ancient family trees intertwined with supernatural lineages, showing centuries of coexistence that predated modern nations. "And our solutions need to respect that history."

Captain Dixon nodded to a corner screen where representatives from smaller, older organizations watched silently: the Vatican's Shadow Office, Tibet's Temple Guardians, Salem's Covenant. They understood what the newer international agencies often forgot - some places had their own ways, tested by time and blood.

"The International Supernatural Treaty requires standardized containment procedures-" the EU representative began, pulling up Article 7 of the 1985 accords.

"Doesn't apply here," Alice cut in, spreading out documents that made several international observers shift uncomfortably. "Daybridge's charter predates your treaty by centuries. Our autonomy was guaranteed by the Blood Compact of 1692, reaffirmed by the Salem Concordat and the Shadow Council's Decree of 1823."

"Times change," argued the Australian representative, his Sydney office showing signs of recent supernatural damage. "Global threats require global responses. The Brisbane Incident proved-"

"Brisbane didn't have our infrastructure," Ethan countered, his eyes flashing wolf-gold as he gestured to their success metrics. "Zero civilian casualties in five years. Show me another jurisdiction with those numbers."

The holographic map pulsed, showing new disturbances emerging worldwide. Each agency's monitoring systems registered the spike, but Daybridge's readings remained steady, protected by layers of both modern and ancient defenses.

"Perhaps," suggested a quiet voice from the Vatican feed, "we should be learning from Daybridge's methods rather than trying to change them." The speaker remained in shadow, but his ancient ring marked him as someone who understood the value of tradition.

Lila opened another volume, this one showing how Daybridge's protective measures had evolved over centuries. "Our solutions grow from our soil," she explained. "You can't transplant them without roots."

"The supernatural ecosystem is delicate," Captain Dixon added. "Each location has its own balance. Standardization could do more harm than good."

Director Tanaka nodded slowly. "In Japan, we understand this. Each region has its own kami, its own yokai. Perhaps..." he paused, looking thoughtful, "perhaps we need a new framework. One that respects local autonomy while facilitating global cooperation."

The screens filled with data as each agency shared their recent challenges: rising supernatural activity, ancient threats reawakening, protective measures failing. But Daybridge's statistics remained constant, its unique blend of old and new maintaining stability.

"We propose an information exchange," Captain Dixon offered. "We share our methods, but each location adapts them to their own supernatural ecosystem. No standardization, no central control."

"The International Oversight Committee won't approve," Dr. Weber warned.

"The Committee is young," the Vatican representative murmured. "Some of us remember older ways. Better ways."

The holographic map shifted again, highlighting success rates across different jurisdictions. Daybridge's numbers stood out clearly, a beacon of stability in increasingly turbulent times.

'We'll need to formalize this," Commander Blackwood said finally. "Create new protocols that respect local autonomy while allowing for international cooperation."

"Already prepared," Alice replied, sharing documents that made several international lawyers look both impressed and concerned. "We call it the Heritage Protocol. Protecting the future by respecting the past."

As the meeting continued, the various screens showing different approaches to supernatural management, it became clear that Daybridge might represent more than just a unique case - it could be a model for a new way forward, one that balanced modern needs with ancient wisdom.

Outside the conference room, Daybridge continued its daily routine, its citizens going about their lives under layers of protection both seen and unseen, old and new, local and universal. A living example of how tradition and progress could coexist, protecting not just a town, but perhaps offering a path forward for a world facing rising supernatural challenges.

~

CHAPTER FIFTEEN

THE SPECTER'S GAME

BACK IN DAYBRIDGE, Ethan and Alice pored over ancient tomes and crumbling manuscripts scattered across the worn oak table in Lila's shop. The air was thick with the scent of protective incense - dragon's blood and sage mingling with rarer substances that made Ethan's enhanced senses tingle. Centuries-old grimoires lay open beside modern PDU case files, while arcane detection equipment hummed quietly in the corner, monitoring supernatural energy fluctuations.

"There has to be something here," Alice muttered, her brow furrowed in concentration as she scanned the faded pages. Her tablet displayed cross-referenced missing persons data alongside historical records of the witch trials. "Some clue to who's behind the abductions, and why they're targeting the descendants of the witch trials."

A map of Daybridge covered one wall, marked with both recent disappearances and historical execution sites. The pattern was becoming clearer - each victim taken from locations that corresponded to ancient points of power, their bloodlines tracing back to specific families from the trials.

Ethan nodded, his own eyes straining to make out the archaic symbols and cryptic verses. His wolf senses detected subtle changes in the shop's magical atmosphere - the protective wards pulsing stronger as night approached. He could feel the frustration mounting within him, the sense that time was running out and the answers they sought were just beyond their grasp.

The latest victim's photo lay on the table - Sarah Mitchell, age 23, whose great-great-great grandmother had been one of the accused. The PDU's supernatural forensics team had found traces of ceremonial magic at the scene, but nothing that matched their official databases.

Suddenly, Lila appeared at his elbow, moving with the silent grace of someone accustomed to walking between worlds. Her emerald eyes glinted with a strange intensity, reflecting candlelight in ways that weren't quite natural. "I may have found something," she said, her voice low and urgent. She laid an ancient leather-bound volume on the table, its pages yellow with age and marked with symbols that seemed to shift under direct observation. "A passage that speaks of a dark ritual, one that could grant the caster power over the spirits of the dead."

Ethan's heart raced at her words, a flicker of hope kindling in his chest. His enhanced senses picked up the subtle change in Lila's heartbeat - whatever she'd found genuinely disturbed her. "What does it say?" he asked, leaning in closer to examine the page she held.

The text was written in multiple languages, some so ancient they predated written history. Magical formulas intertwined with historical accounts, power flowing through the very ink used to record them.

But as he read the ancient words, a chill ran down his spine. The ritual described was one of unspeakable cruelty, a dark and twisted rite that required the sacrifice of innocent blood - specifically, the blood of those who carried the essence of both accused and accuser from the trials. And there, etched in the margins, was a symbol he had seen before - the same mark that had been found at the site of each disappearance.

Alice's tablet chirped, supernatural activity sensors detecting a spike in negative energy. The candles flickered, shadows deepening in the corners of the shop as ancient protections responded to the mere reading of the ritual.

"Lila," he said slowly, his voice heavy with dread, watching as the witch's usually confident demeanor showed cracks of genuine fear. "What is this? What have you brought us into?"

The witch's face was unreadable, her eyes distant and haunted as she traced protective sigils in the air. The temperature in the shop dropped several degrees, frost forming on the windows despite the summer evening outside. "Something I had hoped to never see again," she whispered, pulling another book from a hidden compartment beneath her counter. "A ritual of vengeance, one that could unleash a darkness upon this city unlike anything you've ever known."

She opened the second book, revealing pages written in blood-red ink that still looked wet after centuries. "The Midnight Court isn't just seeking revenge," she continued, her voice taking on the resonance of ancient power. "They're trying to reverse the trials themselves - to unwrite history using the combined power of accuser and accused bloodlines."

Their supernatural detection equipment began registering stronger anomalies across Daybridge. On the wall map, historical execution sites pulsed with renewed energy.

"How many more potential victims?" Alice asked, already pulling up the PDU's genealogical database.

"Too many," Lila replied, spreading out family trees that showed the complex interweaving of Daybridge's bloodlines. "And we're running out of time. The summer solstice approaches, when the barriers between past and present are thinnest."

Ethan's phone buzzed - another disappearance reported, this time from the old courthouse grounds. The game was accelerating, and the stakes were becoming clearer: not just individual lives, but the very fabric of Daybridge's reality hung in the balance.

"We need to move fast," he said, already reaching for his PDU tactical gear. "Contact Dixon, get every available agent on alert. Lila-"

"I'll begin the preparations," she nodded, already gathering materials for protective rituals. "But remember - we're not just fighting people. We're fighting history itself, and history has a way of demanding balance."

As they prepared to leave, the ancient texts seemed to whisper with their own voices, telling stories of old wrongs seeking new vengeance. Daybridge's past and present were colliding, and they stood at the center of the storm.

$\sim$

CHAPTER SIXTEEN

THE SECRET MEETING

THE OLD TOWN hall's basement smelled of mildew and decades of trapped moisture. Ethan's enhanced senses picked up the rapid heartbeats of at least two dozen people behind the heavy oak door. Alice pressed close to his side, her witch's pendant warm against her neck – a warning sign he'd learned to trust.

"Remember," he whispered, "we're just concerned citizens."

They slipped in through the back entrance, finding seats in the shadows of the last row. The basement's low ceiling and exposed pipes created an appropriately clandestine atmosphere for what Ethan recognized as a gathering of Daybridge's oldest families.

Margaret Putnam, whose family name carried the weight of three centuries of Daybridge history, stood at the podium. Her silver hair was pulled back severely, and her fingers gripped a leather-bound book that Ethan's nose identified as ancient vellum.

"Three deaths in two months," Margaret's voice carried authority earned through years on the town council. "All with the same marking we haven't seen since 1692. We can no longer ignore the pattern."

A murmur rippled through the crowd. Ethan spotted Robert Payne, the town's leading architect, and Barbara Henderson, who owned the iron works. The gathering represented Daybridge's power players, both old money and new.

"The protective wards around the town are failing," Margaret continued. "The old families know this. We've felt it."

Robert Payne stood, his modern suit a stark contrast to the room's antiquated setting. "We've been incorporating traditional protections into new constructions – iron nails, rowan wood, salt in the concrete foundations. But it's not enough. Whatever's hunting in Daybridge knows our weaknesses."

"Then we bring back the Order," called out a voice Ethan recognized as belonging to James Proctor, another old family name. "Our ancestors formed it for exactly this purpose. The Society of the Silver Gate."

Ethan's wolf stirred at the name. He'd encountered references to the society in his research – a secret organization of both supernatural and human members dedicated to maintaining the balance in Daybridge. They'd disappeared in the 1960s, or so everyone thought.

"The Order required sacrifices none of us are prepared to make," Barbara Henderson countered, standing. "I propose a modern solution. My foundry can mass-produce the old protections. We can create a network of iron and silver throughout the city. No dark creature could move freely."

Alice's hand found Ethan's knee, squeezing in warning. As a werewolf, this network would severely limit his movement through town. He kept his face carefully neutral.

"And what of those who walk both worlds?" This from Eleanor Bishop, the town's medical examiner who Ethan now suspected knew more about his nature than she'd let on. "Daybridge has always been a sanctuary for all kinds of folk. We can't turn it into a prison."

The debate escalated, splitting the room between traditionalists who wanted to resurrect the old ways and modernists pushing for technological solutions. Ethan watched alliances form and dissolve in real-time, noting who nodded to whom, which families stood together.

Margaret finally raised her hands for silence. "We'll put it to a vote at the next meeting. For now, we need volunteers for night patrols. The old ways demanded watchers. At least in this, we can honor our ancestors."

As people began signing up for patrol shifts, Ethan and Alice exchanged glances. They'd gotten what they came for – confirmation that Daybridge's prominent families were aware of the supernatural threat. But the meeting had raised more questions than answers.

Who would get to decide the town's future? The old families with their secret societies, or the new guard with their iron networks? And how many of these "concerned citizens" knew they were sitting in a room with a werewolf and a hunter?

As they slipped out, Ethan caught Eleanor Bishop watching them. She gave him a slight nod, and he caught the glint of silver at her wrist – an ancient charm he recognized from his family's grimoire.

The game in Daybridge was older and more complicated than he'd imagined, and now he and Alice were pieces on the board whether or not they liked it.

❧

CHAPTER SEVENTEEN

THE BUSINESS DISTRICT

SMILEY SAMUELS' Restaurant Supply had been a fixture of Daybridge's business district since 1923, though the protective sigils hidden in its brick facade were much older. Smiley surveyed the recent changes to his store, carefully disguised to meet both mundane health codes and supernatural safety standards. The new inventory system on sleek tablets tracked silver content alongside prices, with subtle markers indicating which items met PDU specifications for protective gear.

The hardware section had expanded, featuring local craftsmen's "artisanal" iron tools displayed in cases whose "decorative" inlays formed perfect circles of protection. Each piece was hand-forged using traditional methods that just happened to make them effective against certain supernatural threats. The prices were coded - items ending in .13 indicated blessed materials, while .66 marked items specifically designed for defensive purposes.

"Organic herb garden supplies" occupied an entire aisle, organized in a pattern that would look random to health inspectors but made perfect sense to those who knew basic protection spells. Rosemary and sage sat alongside rarer herbs with names carefully translated into their common botanical terms.

56

"The restaurant association's new guidelines are getting strange," his daughter Jenny commented, stacking boxes of salt – now available in "ritual grade" though labeled as "traditional preservation quality." She adjusted her name tag, which contained a subtle protective charm worked into the store's logo.

Through the front windows, Smiley watched members of the Business District Association gathered across the street, architectural plans spread across café tables. They were discussing the installation of "decorative" iron gates across problematic alleys - gates whose designs incorporated ancient protective patterns disguised as historical metalwork.

"They're adapting," Smiley replied, noting how even the most skeptical business owners were now attending the association's "security workshops." The latest surge in supernatural activity had convinced many holdouts. "We all are."

The morning's deliveries included a special order for the new fusion restaurant - their "authentic ceremonial tea set" contained blessed silver worked into the design. The French bistro had ordered "traditional" door handles made of cold-forged iron, while the Italian place wanted "vintage" window treatments with silver-threaded curtains.

Behind the counter, Jenny updated their special orders book - a modern tablet disguised within an ancient ledger whose pages contained centuries of protective knowledge passed down through Daybridge's merchant families. Each entry balanced modern business needs with supernatural defense requirements.

The "Historical Architecture Workshop" filled the renovated community center, whose "energy-efficient" lighting featured bulbs blessed by three different faiths. Ethan watched from the back as Sonja Miller, whose family had been protecting Daybridge businesses since the 1850s, taught residents to disguise protective symbols as colonial decorations.

"These traditional patterns," she explained, showing slides of local architecture, "were very popular in early New England." Her pointer highlighted details that any supernatural entity would recognize as powerful wards. "The historical society particularly recommends these designs for doorways and windows."

Business owners took careful notes, many already planning renovations that would look perfectly ordinary to outside inspectors while significantly upgrading their supernatural defenses. The owner of the new tech startup asked detailed questions about "period-appropriate" office design, his laptop bag marked with carefully modernized protection symbols.

The coffee shop owner demonstrated proper maintenance of "antique" door knockers, teaching subtle movements that would activate their protective properties. His shop's recent "historical renovation" had turned it into one of the most supernaturally secure buildings in the district, all while winning a preservation award.

Ethan's phone buzzed - another DSS warning about unauthorized civilian involvement in supernatural defense. He deleted it without reading, watching instead as Daybridge's business community adapted centuries-old protections to modern needs.

The workshop moved on to discussing "traditional" business practices - inventory systems that tracked supernatural materials alongside regular stock, security cameras positioned to cover both physical and metaphysical threats, employee training that included subtle protective protocols alongside standard safety procedures.

Small business loans from the Daybridge Community Bank now quietly included funds for protective renovations, disguised as historical preservation grants. Insurance policies covered supernatural damage under carefully worded "acts of nature" clauses. Even the Chamber of Commerce's business directory contained coded information about which establishments offered supernatural safe zones.

Through the window, Ethan could see the business district transforming. New awnings incorporated protective geometries, decorative planters contained strategic herb combinations, and shop windows featured displays that doubled as magical barriers. Modern commerce and ancient protection weaving together, hidden in plain sight.

The PDU's monitoring equipment showed the results - a steady decrease in supernatural incidents in commercial areas, even as activity increased elsewhere. The business district was becoming a model of how modern communities could adapt to supernatural realities while maintaining normal operations.

As the workshop concluded, participants left with folders containing both legitimate historical preservation guidelines and carefully disguised protection instructions. Business cards were exchanged, many marked with subtle symbols indicating membership in Daybridge's underground protective networks.

Ethan watched them disperse, returning to shops and offices that increasingly served dual purposes - regular businesses that also formed part of Daybridge's defensive infrastructure. The business district was changing, but then again, it always had. After all, protecting commerce was just good business sense, whether the threats were mundane or supernatural.

～

CHAPTER EIGHTEEN

THE PRICE OF POWER

PRAGUE, DECEMBER 1994

SNOW FELL SILENTLY on the ancient cobblestones of Prague's Old Town, muffling Lila Darkmagic's footsteps as she approached the abandoned church. Gothic spires reached toward a steel-gray sky, while centuries-old gargoyles watched her passage with empty stone eyes. The building had stood here since before the Thirty Years' War, its walls absorbing countless prayers, countless secrets.

And tonight, it would witness one more.

Lila stood before the altar, her breath visible in the frigid air. Moonlight filtered through stained glass windows, casting prismatic shadows across the ancient stones. The words of power still lingered on her lips, bitter as ash, while darkness swirled around her like a living thing. The whispers of the damned grew louder with each passing moment, a cacophony of voices that spoke of power and promises, of debts and desperate bargains.

But even as she fought to maintain her focus on the ritual before her, her mind was drawn inexorably back to another night, another ritual, when she had first stepped onto this path of redemption and regret.

Berlin, 1989

The Wall was falling, and with it, ancient barriers both physical and metaphysical were crumbling. In an abandoned bunker beneath the city, teenage Lila had stood before another altar, her heart racing with anticipation. The forbidden grimoire lay open before her, its pages seeming to pulse with dark energy.

She remembered the thrill as she stepped into the arcane circle, the way the candles had flared with unnatural light. Power had coursed through her veins like liquid fire as she chanted words that should never have been spoken, drunk on the heady sense of invincibility that came with wielding forces beyond mortal understanding.

The circle had blazed with eldrich light, the barriers between worlds growing thin. She had felt unstoppable, immortal, blind to the warnings of her teachers, deaf to the desperate pleas of those who had tried to stop her.

And then, the screams.

The blood.

The sickening realization of what she had unleashed upon the world.

Prague, 1994

Lila shuddered, her hands clenching into fists at her sides. The silver rings on her fingers - each one a seal binding different aspects of the power she had claimed - grew cold against her skin. She had been so young then, so foolish. Power had seemed the answer to everything - to her family's expectations, to the legacy of her bloodline, to her own desperate need to prove herself.

She had believed that the ends justified the means, no matter how terrible. That true power was worth any sacrifice. The old grimoires had promised knowledge, had whispered of secrets that could reshape reality itself.

They hadn't mentioned the cost.

They hadn't spoken of the faces that would haunt her dreams, the innocent lives destroyed by her ambition. They hadn't warned her that power without wisdom, without compassion, was only a curse - a poison that ate away at the soul until nothing remained but ashes and regret.

Now, standing in the ruins of her past, surrounded by the consequences of her actions, she knew the truth. The ritual components laid out before her represented years of searching, of piecing together fragments of forbidden knowledge: blessed silver from monastery vaults, herbs gathered by moonlight from forgotten graves, water from springs that had run dry centuries ago.

Each item was a step toward breaking free, toward severing the bond that tied her to the darkness she had wrought. But even as she prepared for the ritual that might save her soul, she could feel the weight of her guilt bearing down upon her. The faces of those she had sacrificed haunted her every waking moment, their voices joining the whispers that filled the church.

Lila closed her eyes, a single tear tracing its way down her cheek. The marking on her left palm - the sign of her bargain - burned like brands against her skin. She knew that the road ahead would be long and treacherous, that the price of her redemption would be higher than she ever could have imagined.

The powers she had bound would not release their hold easily. They would fight, would try to claim what they believed was rightfully theirs. The darkness she had embraced would try to drag her back, to remind her of the seductive promises that had led her astray.

But she also knew that she had no choice. Too many had suffered for her ambition, too many lives had been shattered by her quest for power. For their sake, for the sake of her own shattered soul, Lila Darkmagic would face the shadows of her past and emerge unbroken on the other side.

Or die trying.

The church bells began to toll midnight as she raised her hands to begin the ritual, ancient words of unbinding rising to meet the darkness she had called forth so long ago. Outside, the snow continued to fall on Prague's ancient streets, covering the tracks of those who walked paths both mortal and mystical, while inside, a woman fought to reclaim her soul from the shadows that had claimed it.

The price of power was high, but the price of redemption would be higher still.

~

CHAPTER NINETEEN
THE QUEEN'S REVENGE

THE CITY of Daybridge lay shrouded in an unnatural darkness, the streets empty and silent as if life had been drained from them. An otherworldly chill hung in the air, having the stench of decay and the whispering echoes of long-forgotten horrors. It was as if the city itself could sense the coming storm, the malevolent forces that even now gathered in the shadows, ready to unleash their unholy fury upon the unsuspecting world.

Deep beneath the streets, in a cavernous chamber lit only by the sickly green glow of ancient runes, a figure cloaked in shadows stood before an altar of blackened stone. It was the Witch Queen, her eyes gleaming with malevolent power as she chanted in a language that had been old when the world was young. Though her former consort, the necromancer Viktor Graves, had been defeated by Detectives Ethan Reeves and Alice Chen, the Witch Queen's thirst for vengeance knew no bounds.

Around her, a sea of shambling corpses swayed and twitched in a grotesque parody of life, their empty eye sockets glowing with the same eerie light that emanated from the altar. This was the heart of her power, the nexus point from which she would soon unleash her army of the undead upon the city above.

As the Witch Queen's chanting reached a fever pitch, the runes on the altar began to pulse with a sickening radiance, the air around them shimmering and warping like a heat haze. With a final, ear-splitting shriek, the ritual reached its climax. A shockwave of necrotic energy exploded outward from the altar, ripping through the chamber with the force of a hurricane.

The Witch Queen threw back her head and laughed, the sound echoing through the chamber like the tolling of a funeral bell. "Behold," she cried, her voice dripping with malevolent glee, "the power of the Bloodline Archive! With this ancient magic at my command, I shall claim Daybridge as my own, and the world shall tremble before me!"

She could feel the barriers between life and death crumbling away, the veil that separated the mortal world from the realm of the damned growing thinner with each passing second. Soon, very soon, her army would march forth to claim the city above, and all would kneel before the might of the Witch Queen.

But even as she savored her upcoming victory, a flicker of movement caught her eye. There, at the edge of the chamber, two figures emerged from the shadows, their faces grim and their weapons ready. The Witch Queen's lips curled back in a snarl of recognition as she beheld the interlopers who dared to stand against her.

Detective Ethan Reeves, his lupine features twisted in a mask of determination and barely contained rage. Alice Chen, her silver blades gleaming in the eerie light as she surveyed the horde of undead with a hunter's keen eye.

Ethan's eyes widened as he saw the ancient tome clutched in the Witch Queen's grasp, its cover pulsing with an otherworldly energy. He recognized it instantly from Lila's descriptions - the Bloodline Archive, the key to the dark power that threatened to engulf the city.

"Alice!" he shouted over the howling of the undead. "The book! We have to get that book!"

The Witch Queen's laughter rang out once more, cruel and mocking. "Foolish mortals," she sneered, her eyes glittering with malice. "You think you can stand against the power of the Bloodline Archive? Against the might of the Witch Queen herself? You will die screaming, and your souls will be mine for all eternity!"

With a gesture, she sent her undead minions surging forward, their grasping claws reaching out to tear the detectives limb from limb. Ethan and Alice met them head-on, their weapons flashing in the eerie light as they fought to reach the altar and the accursed tome that lay on it.

But even as they battled through the horde, they knew that time was running out. The Witch Queen's power was growing with every passing second, and if they didn't stop her soon, all of Daybridge would be lost.

∼

INTERNAL MEMO - DAYBRIDGE PDU

RE: Operational Authority

Priority: HIGH

Recent conflicts with federal DSS agents have required clarification of jurisdictional boundaries. Effective immediately:

1. All supernatural incidents within Daybridge town limits fall under PDU primary jurisdiction

2. DSS agents must report to PDU headquarters before conducting operations

3. Local assets (E. Reeves, A. Chen, L. Darkmagic) retain operational autonomy

4. Emergency response protocols follow PDU guidelines, not federal standards

. . .

NOTE: The Mayor's Office and Town Council fully support this position. Legal precedent established in the 1892 Supernatural Home Rule Act backs our authority.

- Captain J. Dixon

~

CHAPTER TWENTY

THE SCHOOL BOARD MEETING

PRINCIPAL BLANCHE WATSON sat in Daybridge Elementary's conference room, surrounded by carefully "updated" decor that had transformed the space into a subtle protective zone. Ancient symbols were worked into the new carpet's pattern, while the recently installed "energy-efficient" lighting fixtures contained blessed materials.

She fought to keep her voice steady as she reviewed the documents before her. "The playground renovation budget-"

"Will include the suggested materials," Board Member Eleanor Williams interrupted, sliding a folder across the table. The costs listed made Watson's eyes widen - specialized iron alloys for the swing sets, silver-infused paint for the hopscotch courts, carefully sourced stone for the retaining walls. Each item had been carefully coded as "environmentally sustainable" or "historically appropriate."

"This is-"

"Necessary," Williams finished, her tone brooking no argument. As head of the PTA's "Historical Preservation Committee," she had spent months coordinating with other parents who understood Daybridge's unique situation. "The PTA has already raised the funds. Quietly."

She pulled out architectural plans showing playground equipment arranged in distinct patterns - swing sets, slides, and climbing structures positioned to create overlapping circles of protection. Protective symbols were cleverly disguised as decorative elements in the new "artistic" wall murals. The sandbox design incorporated ancient wardstones disguised as decorative border rocks.

"The children-"

"Are more observant than we think," Williams said softly, sharing student artwork that contained surprising insights. A first grader's drawing showed playground shadows that shouldn't exist. A third grader's essay mentioned "funny lights" near the old oak tree. "Better safe than sorry."

Watson studied the maintenance schedules - regular equipment checks that would double as ward renewals. The "safety inspections" included testing supernatural barriers. Even the landscaping plan served dual purposes, with protective herbs mixed into the decorative plantings.

"The kindergarten teacher reported another incident last week," Williams continued, sharing a carefully worded incident report. "Three students noticed something by the fence line. Something that shouldn't have been there."

The security camera footage showed the children instinctively moving away from that section of the playground, gathering in areas that, Watson now realized, corresponded to stronger protective zones. They had sensed the danger before any adults noticed.

"We've had more transfer students this year," Watson noted, reviewing enrollment files that showed an increasing number of families moving to Daybridge from other supernaturally active areas. "Their parents chose this district specifically."

"Exactly," Williams agreed. "They know what's out there. And they expect us to protect their children."

The renovation plans included updates to other areas as well. The cafeteria would get new "traditional" silverware with subtle protective properties. Library shelves would be reinforced with blessed wood. Even the music room's "acoustic improvements" incorporated protective elements.

"The budget committee-"

"Has already approved it," Williams assured her, sharing documentation that showed how carefully the costs had been distributed across various standard improvement funds. "The superintendent signed off this morning. We're calling it the 'Heritage Learning Environment Initiative.'"

Watson examined the construction timeline, noting how it aligned with naturally stronger protective periods. The major work would be done during summer break, when the school's existing wards were traditionally renewed.

"And the teachers?"

"Will receive updated safety training," Williams explained, sharing a professional development schedule that cleverly combined standard protocols with supernatural awareness. "We're packaging it as 'traditional emergency response methods.'"

The plans showed how every aspect had been considered. The new playground design would channel children away from vulnerable areas while making safe zones naturally appealing. Games would be subtly adjusted to keep students within protected spaces. Even the recess schedule had been optimized around supernatural activity patterns.

"The other elementary schools-"

"Are implementing similar measures," Williams confirmed. "The whole district is upgrading, one 'renovation' at a time."

Watson looked out the conference room window at the current playground, seeing it with new eyes. Children played normally, but she noticed how they unconsciously avoided certain areas, clustered in safer spaces. They sensed things adults often missed.

"When do we begin?"

"Construction starts next month," Williams replied, sharing the contractor list - all local firms with long histories in Daybridge. "The children's safety can't wait."

As they continued reviewing plans, Watson noticed how the afternoon shadows moved across the playground. The new design would ensure those shadows never fell quite the same way again, though only those who knew what to look for would understand why.

The children of Daybridge would play, laugh, and learn, protected by carefully disguised measures that bridged ancient wisdom and modern safety standards. Their playground would stand as another example of how the town adapted, protecting its youngest citizens with methods hidden in plain sight.

This was Daybridge, after all, where even hopscotch courts could serve as circles of protection, and where keeping children safe meant understanding that some threats wouldn't appear on standard safety inspection forms.

CHAPTER TWENTY-ONE

A HAUNTING ALLIANCE

LILA'S HEART raced as she slipped through the shadows of the
Necropolis, the stench of death and decay thick in her nostrils. She had
followed the trail of dark magic to this ancient burial ground, knowing
that the Bloodline Archive lay hidden somewhere within its crumbling
crypts and mausoleums.

For weeks, she had been searching for the accursed book, the key to
breaking the soul bond that still tied her to the dark magic she had
once wielded. Every moment she spent bound to that darkness was a
torment, the twisted desires and blackened thoughts seeping into her
mind like poison.

But now, at last, she was close. She could feel the tome's presence like a
physical weight upon her soul, its dark power calling out to her across
the centuries. She knew the risks, knew that to even touch the book
was to court madness and damnation. But what choice did she have?
The alternative was a fate far worse than death.

As she picked her way through the maze of tombstones and monu-
ments, Lila's thoughts turned to Ethan and Alice. She had heard whispers of their investigation, knew that they too were closing in on the
truth behind the kidnappings. A part of her longed to reach out to

them, to warn them of the dangers they faced. But she couldn't risk it, couldn't bear the thought of dragging them into her own personal hell.

Suddenly, a sound echoed through the graveyard, shattering the sepulchral silence. Footsteps, heavy and purposeful, drawing ever closer. Lila froze, her hand tightening around the hilt of her athame. She knew that tread, knew the aura of darkness that accompanied it like a shroud.

A figure stepped out from behind a mausoleum, cloaked in shadow, their face obscured by a deep hood. In their grasp, the Bloodline Archive pulsed with malevolent energy, its ancient pages rustling in the fetid breeze.

"Lila Darkmagic," the figure rasped, their voice like the grating of stone on stone. "I knew you would come. You always were drawn to power, weren't you?"

Lila's eyes narrowed, her heart pounding in her chest. "Who are you?" she demanded, her voice ringing out across the graveyard. "And what do you want with the Bloodline Archive?"

The figure laughed, a sound like the rattling of bones in a crypt. "I am the Witch Queen," they declared, throwing back their hood to reveal a face that was little more than a skull, with glowing embers for eyes. "And the Tome is the key to my vengeance, the instrument of my wrath against those who wronged me so long ago."

Lila felt a chill run down her spine at the Witch Queen's words, the dark magic that emanated from her like a physical force. "I can't let you do this," she said, her voice trembling with a mixture of fear and determination. "The Tome's power is too great, too terrible. It will consume you, just as it consumed me."

The Witch Queen's skeletal grin widened, her ember-eyes flaring with malevolent glee. "Oh, but I am not like you, little necromancer," she hissed. "I embrace the darkness, revel in its power. And with the Tome in my grasp, I will be unstoppable."

She raised the Bloodline Archive, her voice rising in a chant that made the ground tremble beneath their feet. Dark energy crackled around her, coalescing into a swirling vortex of shadow and flame. From the depths of the Necropolis, the dead rose, their skeletal forms clawing their way out of the earth to answer their mistress's call.

Lila stood her ground, her athame drawn and her eyes blazing with determination. She knew that she was outmatched, that even with all her skill and power, she could not hope to defeat the Witch Queen alone.

But she also knew that she had to try, had to do everything in her power to stop the monster she had unwittingly unleashed upon the world. For the innocent lives at stake, for her own shattered soul, Lila Darkmagic would see this through to the bitter end.

Raising her blade, she charged forward, a battle cry tearing itself from her throat as she hurled herself into the fray. The shadows reached out to claim her, but she would not yield. Not now, not ever. The price of vengeance would be paid in blood and fire, and Lila would gladly be the one to pay it.

Even as the hordes of undead closed in around her, their grasping claws tearing at her flesh, Lila fought on. She would not rest until the Bloodline Archive was in her grasp, until the dark magic that bound her was severed once and for all.

For in the grim and haunted world of Daybridge, there could be no peace, no respite from the darkness. There was only the fight, the eternal struggle against the shadows that threatened to consume them all.

And Lila Darkmagic would not stop fighting, not until her last breath was drawn and her last drop of blood was spilled. For she was a witch, a guardian of the light in a world of darkness, and she would not rest until the innocent were safe once more.

CHAPTER TWENTY-TWO

THE OCCULT BOOKSHOP

THE BELL above Madame Noir's Arcane Acquisitions jingled discordantly as Ethan and Alice entered the narrow shop. The sound wasn't brass – Ethan's sensitive ears recognized the distinct tone of bone striking bone. Wind chimes made from finger bones. Old magic.

"Your timing is impeccable," came a voice from somewhere behind the towering shelves. "The tea just finished steeping."

Ethan navigated through the maze of bookstacks, his nostrils filled with competing scents: aging leather, foxed paper, dried herbs, and something else – something that made his wolf stir uneasily. Dragon's blood resin, he realized. The whole shop was warded.

They found Madame Noir in a small reading nook, pouring tea into three mismatched cups. She was younger than her voice suggested, maybe forty, with tight copper curls and skin the color of well-worn mahogany. Multiple rings adorned her fingers, each humming with its own subtle power.

"Detective Reeves," she smiled, revealing teeth that were just slightly too sharp to be human. "And Miss Chen. I've been expecting you both since the second body turned up."

Alice tensed beside him. They hadn't mentioned the murders to anyone outside the investigation.

"Please," Madame Noir gestured to two worn leather armchairs, "The tea helps with the conversation we're about to have. Ceylon black, with a touch of yarrow for clarity."

Ethan took his seat, noting how the chair seemed to mold itself to his frame. "We're looking for information about-"

"The Bloodline Archive," she finished, sipping her tea. "Along with half of Daybridge, it seems. Never seen such a run on protective literature. Had three different people ask about it just this morning – though they were far less qualified to handle such knowledge."

She rose, moving to a locked cabinet behind her desk. The keys at her belt jangled – iron, silver, and what looked like bone – as she selected one.

"The town is scared," Alice said, warming her hands around her teacup. "People are starting to remember the old stories."

"Remember? Oh, my dear, they never forgot." Madame Noir returned with a leather-bound journal; its pages yellow with age. "Daybridge was founded by those who understood the true nature of the world. The veil between worlds is naturally thin here. It's why the first settlers chose this location."

She opened the journal carefully. "This belonged to Jonathan Noir, my great-great-grandfather. He was the town's first official chronicler of the unusual. And unofficial mediator between the human and supernatural communities."

Ethan leaned forward, catching sight of detailed sketches – creatures he recognized and others he'd only heard whispered about in the darker corners of the supernatural world.

"The Bloodline Archive isn't just a book," Madame Noir continued. "It's a key. The original settlers of Daybridge created it as both a weapon and a shield. But like most powerful tools, it was deemed too dangerous to keep in one piece."

"They broke it apart," Alice breathed, her hunter's intuition picking up the threads. "The families each took a piece..."

"Seven families, seven fragments," Madame Noir nodded. "Each containing a portion of the knowledge and power. Your murders? Someone's trying to reassemble it."

Ethan's wolf growled softly. "The victims – were they from the original families?"

"Better." Madame Noir turned several pages in the journal. "They were guardians. Each of the seven families appointed one person per generation to protect their fragment. Your killer is hunting guardians."

She paused, studying them both. "But you already suspected that, didn't you, Detective? Your own family was one of the seven."

The revelation hit Ethan like a physical blow. His grandmother's stories, the old chest in the attic he'd never been allowed to open, his father's insistence that he learn the old ways even after he'd been turned...

"Five guardians remain," Madame Noir said softly. "And the killer's getting bolder. The protective wards around town are failing because they were never meant to work independently. The Bloodline Archive was the keystone that held Daybridge's defenses together."

She stood, moving to one of the towering shelves. "Business has been extraordinary lately. Everyone wanting protection, seeking answers." She pulled down several volumes. "These might help you understand what you're dealing with. Consider them a loan... and a warning."

As she stacked the books on the table, Ethan caught titles in languages he recognized and others he didn't: "Guardians of the Veil," "Blood Wards and Boundary Magic," "The Seven Seals of Daybridge."

"The killer isn't working alone," Madame Noir said as they gathered the books. "Old magic like this requires a circle. Find one, you'll find the others."

At the door, she caught Ethan's arm. Her rings felt cold against his skin. "Detective, when your grandmother visits next week, send her my regards. She still owes me a game of cards... and a very important conversation about family history."

Outside, the autumn air felt sharp after the shop's incense-heavy atmosphere. Alice clutched the books to her chest, her face pale. "Ethan, your grandmother... is she...?"

"A guardian?" He stared at the shop's window, where crystals and dried herbs swayed in a breeze he couldn't feel. "I think I need to make a phone call."

The bell chimed behind them – bone striking bone – a sound that now seemed less like a welcome and more like a warning.

❧

CHAPTER TWENTY-THREE
ANOTHER OCCULT BOOKSHOP

ETHAN HESITATED at the entrance of "The Grimoire's Heart," his hand hovering over the shop's brass doorknob. Through the smudged storefront window, crystals caught the late afternoon light, casting prismatic patterns on stacks of leather-bound books.

"Something wrong?" Alice asked, adjusting her messenger bag.

"Just getting a read on the place," he murmured, his enhanced senses picking up layers of scents: sage, sandalwood, old paper, and beneath it all, the distinct metallic tang of protective wards. "This isn't just for tourists. These are serious defenses."

The door creaked open before either of them could reach for it. A woman's voice drifted out from the darkness within: "Please, Detective Reeves, do come in. The protective circles won't bite – though I can't say the same for some of the books."

They exchanged glances before stepping inside. The shop was larger than it appeared from the street, with shelves stretching up to a ceiling lost in shadows. Books were arranged not by author or title, but by phases of the moon, evidenced by the silver symbols marking each section.

The owner emerged from between two towering bookcases, her silver-streaked black hair tied back with what Ethan recognized as blessed cord. She moved with the fluid grace of someone who wasn't entirely human, though he couldn't pin down her exact nature.

"Iris Vale," she introduced herself, dark eyes studying them both. "Though most folks around here just call me the Keeper. You're here about the Bloodline Archive."

It wasn't a question.

"How did you—" Alice began.

"When you've been manning the supernatural checkout desk as long as I have, you learn to read the signs." Iris gestured for them to follow her deeper into the shop. "Plus, you're the third group this week asking about it. Though the others weren't quite as..." she glanced at Ethan, "qualified to handle such information."

They arrived at a reading area furnished with mismatched Victorian chairs and a table that looked carved from a single piece of ancient oak. Various artifacts decorated the space: a crystal ball that seemed to hold actual storm clouds, a dagger with runes that shifted along its blade, and a mirror that showed no reflections.

"Please, sit," Iris said, pulling a heavy ledger from a nearby shelf. "I've been keeping track of the shop's visitors lately. The pattern is... concerning."

She opened the ledger, revealing pages of elegant script. "In the past month alone, I've had over fifty requests for books on protective sigils. Another thirty-seeking information on warding techniques. Even had the mayor's wife in here yesterday, asking about blood wards – though she tried to play it off as 'historical research.'"

"The murders are making people nervous," Ethan observed.

"It's more than that." Iris ran a finger down the ledger's entries. "People are remembering things they've spent generations trying to forget. Old family histories. Ancient pacts. The real reason Daybridge was founded."

Alice leaned forward. "What do you mean?"

Iris closed the ledger with a snap. "This town wasn't built here by accident. The earliest settlers chose this location because of what lies beneath it – ley lines intersecting at points of power. Daybridge sits at a crossroads between worlds."

She stood, moving to a locked cabinet behind her desk. The key she used seemed to be made of dark glass that absorbed light.

"The Bloodline Archive was created to harness and protect these convergence points," she continued, retrieving a slim volume bound in what Ethan's nose told him was definitely not ordinary leather. "But it was also a warning system. When the barriers between worlds grew thin, the Tome would alert its keepers."

"And now those barriers are weakening," Alice said softly.

"Precisely." Iris placed the book on the table. "This is just a commentary on the Tome, written in 1876 by a scholar named Edmund Pierce. The actual Tome... well, that's what your killer is after, isn't it?"

Ethan felt his wolf stir at her words. "How much do you know about these murders?"

"I know the victims were all connected to the old families. I know the symbols found at the crime scenes match certain passages in the original Tome. And I know—" she fixed Ethan with a penetrating stare, "— that you're not just here as a detective."

She turned to a specific page in Pierce's book. "The Bloodline Archive contains secrets that could either protect this town or tear it apart. Your killer isn't working alone. Old magic like this requires a circle – usually seven practitioners. Find one, you'll find the others."

"Any suggestions on where to start looking?" Ethan asked.

Iris smiled, revealing teeth that gleamed like opals. "Start with the living. Work backward. The old families keep detailed records – when you know where to look." She pulled a business card from her sleeve and handed it to Alice. "If you need more specific guidance, come back on a waning moon. Bring silver coins minted before 1964. Knowledge has its price."

As they prepared to leave, Iris caught Ethan's arm. Her touch sent a jolt of energy through him that made his wolf hackles rise.

"Detective," she said quietly, "be careful who you trust. Daybridge's foundations run deep, but some of the oldest pillars are rotting from within. And remember – sometimes the most dangerous books are the ones that find you."

Outside, the setting sun painted the sky in shades of blood orange. Alice studied the business card, which seemed to show different text depending on how she held it.

"Well," she said, "that was…"

"Informative?" Ethan suggested, still feeling the lingering energy from Iris's touch.

"I was going to say terrifying." Alice tucked the card away. "Do you think she's trustworthy?"

Ethan looked back at the shop window. For a moment, he could have sworn he saw not their reflections, but seven shadowy figures standing in a circle.

Then he blinked, and there was nothing but crystals and books.

"Trustworthy? "No," he said finally. "But useful? Absolutely. And right now, we need all the help we can get."

The sun dipped below the horizon, and somewhere in the distance, church bells began to toll. Neither of them mentioned that it wasn't anywhere near the hour.

～

CHAPTER TWENTY-FOUR
A FATEFUL DISCOVERY

THE UNIVERSITY LIBRARY'S sub-basement hadn't seen visitors in decades. Nadia's flashlight beam caught dust motes that danced like fairy lights, her steps echoing against century-old tile. The Miskatonic Collection's restricted section had led her here, following references in a witch's grimoire from 1892.

Her hands trembled as she consulted Elizabeth's journal:

"The Daughters of the Dark Moon weren't just a coven. They were guardians, chosen by the earth itself to maintain the balance. When the Caligari Cataclysm threatened to break through, they sacrificed every-thing to seal the breach."

The beam of her flashlight caught something on the wall – a symbol carved into the brick. A crescent moon intersected by three stars, like the diagram she'd found in Professor Jones's thesis about Daybridge's founding families.

"Found you," she whispered.

Her fingers traced the symbol, feeling warmth pulse beneath her touch. The wall shuddered, ancient mechanisms groaning to life.

Bricks rearranged themselves, revealing a narrow passage that descended into darkness.

Nadia checked her phone – no signal, as expected. She'd told Alice she was doing research tonight but hadn't mentioned where. The hunter would be furious when she found out, but some paths had to be walked alone.

The passage led to a circular chamber that took her breath away. Thirteen pillars of black stone surrounded a central altar, each carved with flowing script that seemed to move in her flashlight beam. The air hummed with dormant power.

"The Circle of the Dark Moon," she breathed, recognizing it from her research. "Their sacred space."

The altar bore the same crescent moon symbol, but larger, more elaborate. Crystals were embedded in the stone at precise points, creating a pattern she recognized from her ancestor's drawings.

Her flashlight flickered, then died. But the chamber wasn't dark. The crystals began to glow with a soft blue light, responding to her presence.

"Blood calls to blood," she remembered Elizabeth's words. "The Daughters always return."

On the altar lay a single object – a bronze pendant in the shape of a crescent moon, blackened with age. When Nadia lifted it, images flooded her mind:

Thirteen witches standing where she stood now, channeling power through the earth's ley lines. A darkness pressing against reality's edges, trying to break through. The witches joining hands, their combined power flowing into the pendant, creating a key to lock away the growing darkness.

The last image hit her like a physical blow: Elizabeth Marsh, accepting the pendant from the coven's dying leader, swearing an oath to protect it until it was needed again.

Nadia gasped as the vision released her. The pendant pulsed warmly in her hand, recognizing her bloodline, her purpose.

"So that's what you've been hiding down here."

She spun to find Alice in the doorway, looking both worried and impressed. "How did you—"

"You really think I wouldn't put a tracking device on you after last time?" Alice stepped into the chamber; her eyes wide as she took in the ancient witch-work. "The Daughters' sanctuary. We thought it was lost."

"Not lost," Nadia held up the pendant. "Waiting. The power they used to seal the breach – they stored it in here. They knew someday the darkness would try again."

"And they knew a Marsh would find it." Alice touched one of the pillars reverently. "The old families kept more secrets than we realized."

The crystals pulsed brighter as Alice neared them, responding to her natural magic." This isn't just a ritual space. It's a battery, storing power gathered over centuries."

"Power we're going to need." Nadia slipped the pendant around her neck, feeling its energy merge with her own. "The coven that's been causing trouble topside? They're trying to undo the original seal. But they don't understand what they're dealing with."

"And you do?"

"I'm starting to." Nadia touched the nearest pillar, watching symbols light up under her fingers. "The Daughters knew something was coming. Something big. They prepared for it; left us the tools we'd need."

"Us?"

"Look at the pillars, Alice. Thirteen of them. Thirteen witches. The original circle needs to be reformed."

Understanding dawned in Alice's eyes. "A new coven."

"To face an old darkness." Nadia pulled out her phone, already composing a message to Ethan. "But first, we need to find the others. The descendants of the original thirteen. The power's been passed down through bloodlines, whether they know it or not."

The pendant grew warm against her chest as Alice touched it, adding her own magic to its stored power. The chamber responded, crystals blazing brighter, ancient energies awakening.

"Your ancestor left you more than just journals," Alice said softly. "She left you a legacy."

"She left us a weapon," Nadia corrected, thinking of the visions, the warnings, the price of power. "Now we just need to learn how to use it."

Above them, thunder rolled across Daybridge's sky. The witching hour approached, and in her blood, Nadia felt the old power stirring. The Daughters of the Dark Moon had protected this town once before.

Now it was their turn.

CHAPTER TWENTY-FIVE

THE TOWN MEETING

DAYBRIDGE's historic town hall stood as a testament to centuries of adaptation. Its recent "renovations" went far beyond the official permits would suggest. Iron-reinforced doors gleamed with subtle blessed inlays, while new windows perfectly aligned with the ley lines that crisscrossed beneath the town. The "energy-efficient" lighting system incorporated crystals that responded to supernatural threats, and the fresh paint contained traces of materials that would make any malevolent entity uncomfortable.

Mayor James Thompson stood at the podium, which had been carefully positioned at the intersection of three protective circles hidden beneath the new carpeting. The wood itself came from an ancient oak that had once served as a focal point for the town's earliest wards. Behind him, the town seal had been subtly modified, its traditional design now incorporating symbols of protection that most viewers would dismiss as decorative flourishes.

The crowd filled every seat, a mix of old families and newer residents who had chosen Daybridge for reasons they couldn't quite explain. Business owners checked their phones while fingering protective charms disguised as traditional jewelry. Parents reviewed school renovation proposals while their children drew pictures that sometimes showed more than they should. Even the local tech startup founders had adapted their laptops sporting cases marked with modernized versions of ancient wards.

"Our heritage preservation initiatives have been successful," Mayor Thompson announced, as Lila, seated in the back row, noticed the fresh protection circles painted beneath the new carpets. Their pattern formed a complex grid that connected to older wards laid down by the town's founders. The "historical restoration" budget had covered much more than simple maintenance.

From her position, Lila could see how the renovations had transformed the building into a nexus of protective energy. The new chandelier crystals caught and redirected harmful energies, while the "decorative" wall sconces contained blessed metals that would react to supernatural threats. Even the air conditioning system had been modified, its vents positioned to maintain a constant flow of blessed air.

"But there's more work to be done," the mayor continued, clicking through his presentation. The projector hummed, its "upgraded" bulb casting light that somehow made protective symbols more visible to those who knew what to look for.

The infrastructure plans appeared on screen, carefully coded to appear as routine upgrades to those who didn't know better. Streets would be repaved with materials that included protective elements. The water system would be "modernized" with filters that did more than remove physical contaminants. New street lights would form patterns that created barriers against supernatural threats.

Ethan, seated near the emergency exit (its frame recently reinforced with cold-forged iron), studied the plans with his enhanced vision. He could see how each "improvement" connected to existing protective measures, strengthening the town's defenses while maintaining its appearance as a typical New England community.

Alice, positioned strategically near the center of the room, made notes on her tablet, cross-referencing the proposed changes with PDU threat assessments. The plans showed careful coordination between mundane improvements and supernatural defense - new parking structures would double as containment areas, while park renovations would create safe zones disguised as picnic areas.

The true pattern emerged as they studied the plans - Daybridge was methodically transforming itself into a fortress, its very architecture becoming a weapon against darkness. Each street, building, and public space was being carefully modified to serve dual purposes, protecting its citizens while maintaining normal appearances.

"The historical society has approved all proposed changes," announced Michelle Cruise, head of the preservation committee, her antique brooch containing wards passed down through generations. "These improvements will help maintain our town's unique character."

The "unique character" she referred to went far beyond architectural style. Maps showed how each phase of construction would strengthen different aspects of the town's defenses. The new community center would anchor protective energies on the east side, while "traffic flow improvements" would actually channel supernatural threats away from residential areas.

Questions from the audience revealed how deeply the knowledge ran in Daybridge. A question about street lighting patterns masked concerns about nocturnal entities. Discussions of playground renovations included subtle references to protecting children from more than physical harm. Even queries about parking regulations contained coded language about maintaining protective boundaries.

"The budget has been allocated," Mayor Thompson continued, sharing financial reports that disguised supernatural defense costs as standard municipal expenses. "Work will begin next month, starting with the historic district."

The "historic district" improvements would reinforce the town's oldest protections while adding modern innovations. Technology and tradition would merge, creating defenses that could adapt to evolving threats while honoring centuries of accumulated wisdom.

As the meeting continued, Lila observed how naturally Daybridge's citizens discussed their town's transformation. They debated color schemes that would incorporate protective sigils, argued about playground designs that would keep children within safe zones, and suggested modifications to parking structures that would double as supernatural containment areas.

This was how Daybridge had always survived - by adapting, by hiding its true nature in plain sight, by turning every aspect of ordinary life into a defense against extraordinary threats. The town was becoming something unique: a modern community built on ancient foundations, where every brick and beam served to protect its people from forces they increasingly couldn't ignore.

The meeting concluded with a detailed construction timeline, carefully planned around supernatural cycles and natural power fluctuations. As residents filed out, discussing what appeared to be routine civic matters, Ethan, Alice, and Lila exchanged knowing looks. Daybridge was preparing for whatever darkness might come, transforming itself one "renovation" at a time into something far more than a typical New England town.

It was becoming a bastion against the darkness, its defenses woven into every aspect of daily life, invisible to outsiders but increasingly apparent to those who called it home. The town meeting had been more than civic duty - it was another step in Daybridge's centuries-long evolution, adapting to face whatever threats the future might bring.

CHAPTER TWENTY-SIX

UNDERGROUND NETWORK

THE PDU's underground command center, built within centuries-old tunnels beneath Daybridge, represented a fusion of modern technology and ancient protection. Blessed servers processed data while wardstones hummed in the walls. Screens displayed supernatural activity reports from allied organizations worldwide, each operating according to their local traditions:

Salem's Witch Watch reported increased activity around historical sites, their modern monitoring systems incorporating centuries of magical knowledge. New Orleans' Voodoo Enforcement Division shared data on dimensional disturbances, their reports mixing scientific analysis with traditional wisdom. Prague's Golem Control Unit tracked energy patterns through the old Jewish Quarter, using both cutting-edge sensors and ancient Kabbalistic methods.

Officer Sarah Rodriguez, whose family had served in supernatural law enforcement for three generations, monitored the secure communications channels. Her workstation combined standard police equipment with tools passed down through her bloodline. "Underground network's picking up chatter," she reported, cross-referencing reports from dozens of local agencies worldwide. "Something big's brewing. Not just here - everywhere."

The global feed showed disturbing patterns: increased activity at historical sites, dimensional anomalies in major cities, ancient artifacts awakening after centuries of dormancy. Each location reported the phenomena in their own way, using frameworks developed over generations of dealing with supernatural forces.

"The old powers are waking," Lila confirmed, connecting via secure channels with other archivists - the keepers of supernatural knowledge in communities worldwide. Her screen showed conversations in multiple languages, mixing modern encryption with ancient protective protocols. "But each place needs to handle it their way. Cookie-cutter federal responses will just make things worse."

Institutional Conflict

The DSS regional headquarters gleamed with modern efficiency, its sterile conference room a stark contrast to Daybridge's organic approach to supernatural defense. Director Matthews, his pressed suit and polished shoes reflecting federal standardization, slammed his fist on the conference table.

"You can't just ignore federal guidelines! The President himself signed Executive Order 13666 establishing our authority-"

"With all due respect," Captain Dixon replied, his calm demeanor masking steel resolve, "Daybridge's supernatural defense infrastructure was established before this country existed. Our methods-"

"Are dangerous and unpredictable!" Matthews interrupted, pulling up standardized risk assessment forms. "A werewolf as lead investigator? A hunter working officially with local law enforcement? An archive of dark magic accessible to civilians?"

His screen displayed federal protocols - standardized responses designed to be implemented anywhere. But each page showed the fundamental disconnect between bureaucratic standardization and supernatural reality.

"All of which have kept our town safe for generations," Dixon countered, spreading out historical records showing Daybridge's success rate against supernatural threats. "While your standardized procedures led to the Chicago Disaster last month."

The mention of Chicago made Matthews flinch. The federal response there had ignored local supernatural dynamics, trying to impose standard procedures on unique situations. The results had been catastrophic.

Global Implications

The PDU's situation room buzzed with activity as the global map displayed supernatural hot spots. Red dots pulsed in major cities worldwide - London's ancient wards straining, Tokyo's technological-mystical defenses detecting anomalies, Cairo's millennia-old protections responding to new threats.

But Daybridge glowed with a unique pattern, its combination of traditional methods and modern adaptation creating a distinctive signature. The town's approach had caught the attention of supernatural defense agencies worldwide.

"Other agencies are watching us," Alice noted, analyzing reports from international observers. Communities facing similar challenges studied how Daybridge balanced federal requirements with local traditions, modern technology with ancient wisdom.

"The federal boys want control," Ethan growled, his enhanced senses detecting subtle changes in the supernatural atmosphere. "But they don't understand. Each community's relationship with the supernatural is unique. Try to standardize it..."

"And you break what works," Lila finished, gesturing to the Archive's extensive records. "The Archive shows how different places developed different solutions. Forcing everyone to follow the same playbook is asking for disaster."

The screens showed how various communities handled supernatural threats: Montreal's ice mages working with modern emergency services, Venice's water-based defenses incorporating centuries of maritime tradition, Istanbul's multilayered approach reflecting millennia of accumulated wisdom.

Each location had developed methods suited to their unique history, population, and supernatural ecosystem. Federal standardization threatened these carefully evolved systems, trying to replace organic local responses with one-size-fits-all solutions.

The global feed continued updating: Mexico City's ancient Aztec wards activating beneath modern streets, Sydney's dreamtime protections responding to new threats, Berlin's post-war supernatural defenses detecting unusual patterns. Each community faced similar challenges but approached them through their own cultural and historical lens.

"We're not just fighting supernatural threats," Alice observed, studying the patterns. "We're fighting for the right to face them our own way."

The situation room's displays showed the complexity of the challenge: maintaining effective local responses while dealing with federal oversight, preserving traditional methods while incorporating modern innovations, protecting communities while respecting their unique approaches to supernatural defense.

Daybridge's experience could show a way forward - demonstrating how communities could maintain their traditional methods while adapting to modern realities, how local knowledge could complement rather than conflict with federal resources, how centuries of accumulated wisdom could work alongside contemporary technology.

The world was watching, as communities everywhere faced similar challenges. How Daybridge balanced these competing demands could influence supernatural defense policies globally, showing a way to preserve local traditions while meeting modern challenges.

The underground command center continued monitoring worldwide supernatural activity, its very existence representing the balance Daybridge sought to maintain - ancient tunnels housing modern technology, traditional wards protecting digital equipment, centuries of local knowledge informing contemporary responses to eternal threats.

CHAPTER TWENTY-SEVEN

THE FINAL SACRIFICE

THE OLD FOUNDRY'S iron doors groaned as Ethan and Alice approached. Behind them, Lila Darkmagic clutched the Bloodline Archive to her chest, its pages thrumming with dark energy that made Ethan's wolf stir restlessly beneath his skin. Already, he could feel the familiar itch of impending transformation - his muscles twitching, bones aching with the need to shift.

"She's channeling power from the ley lines," Lila whispered, her fingers tracing the book's ancient symbols. "The Witch Queen's trying to complete what she started centuries ago."

Ethan's senses were becoming sharper with each passing moment. The coppery scent of blood mixed with ozone made his nostrils flare. His teeth ached, canines threatening to lengthen. He could hear five distinct heartbeats from within - the victims, their pulses racing with terror.

Inside, the foundry was a maze of rusted machinery and writhing shadows. Sweat beaded on Ethan's forehead as he fought to maintain control. His vision shifted between human and wolf, the darkness becoming clearer, shapes more defined. His hands curled into fists, nails already sharpening into claws.

They found her in the central chamber, resplendent in her darkness. The Witch Queen stood within a circle of power, drawing life force from five bound descendants of the original accusers. Their screams sent shockwaves through Ethan's transforming body, the adrenaline spike pushing him closer to the edge.

"Ravenna!" Alice's voice cut through the charged air; her crossbow raised.

The Queen turned, lips curling into a cruel smile. "The hunter, the wolf, and the little witch who thinks she can control powers beyond her understanding." Her eyes fixed on the Bloodline Archive. "Bring me my book, child, and I might let you live."

Ethan's spine cracked audibly as it began to reshape itself. He dropped to one knee, muscles spasming. The wolf wasn't waiting for the full moon tonight - it was clawing its way out, driven by the presence of such powerful magic and the need to protect his companions.

"The Archive was never yours," Lila replied, opening it to a marked page. "It belongs to all the wronged."

The first exchange of spells lit up the foundry like daylight, and it was the final trigger Ethan needed. His transformation exploded forth in a symphony of cracking bones and tearing flesh. His clothes shredded as his body expanded, dark fur bursting from his skin in waves. His face elongated into a powerful muzzle filled with razor-sharp teeth. His hands and feet twisted into massive paws tipped with gleaming claws.

The massive silver black wolf that emerged was larger than any natural animal, muscles rippling beneath thick fur, eyes gleaming with both human intelligence and primal fury. His howl shook dust from the rafters as Alice's bolts flew true and Lila's magic met the Queen's in spectacular collisions of energy.

In this form, Ethan could see the patterns of magic swirling around them, could smell the ancient power emanating from both the Archive and the Queen. His enhanced senses made him the perfect warrior for this battle - immune to many of the Queen's spells while having the strength to tear through her magical barriers.

The wolf launched itself into battle with savage grace, moving in perfect coordination with his human allies. Three different kinds of power - primal, martial, and magical - united against the darkness that threatened their town.

CHAPTER TWENTY-EIGHT
THE NECROMANCER'S GAMBIT

THE BATTLE TRANSFORMED the foundry into chaos incarnate. The massive silver black wolf that was Ethan tore through summoned spirits while Alice's blessed bolts disrupted the Queen's defenses. Lila wielded the Archive like a conductor's baton, its magic responding to her will in ways the Queen hadn't expected.

"The book recognizes its true purpose!" Lila shouted over the magical thunder. "Not vengeance - justice!"

The Witch Queen snarled; centuries of hatred made manifest. "Justice? There is no justice but what we take!" She gestured, and the bound descendants screamed anew.

Ethan's wolf form launched itself through a gap in her defenses, while Alice's bolts forced her to divide her attention. Lila began a counter-ritual, the Archive's pages turning by themselves as ancient words of power spilled from her lips.

"The true power was never in hatred," Lila continued, her voice gaining strength. "It was in the bonds between the innocent!"

The Archive blazed with sudden light as Ethan's jaws closed on the Queen's arm, breaking her connection to the ritual. Alice's next bolt struck true, piercing the Queen's shoulder. The three worked in perfect synchronization - physical, martial, and magical powers combined.

As her ritual collapsed, the Witch Queen screamed in fury and desperation. "You cannot undo three centuries of hatred!"

"Watch us," Lila replied, raising the Archive high. Its light joined with Ethan's primal strength and Alice's unwavering goal. The Queen's own magic turned inward, consumed by the very powers she had tried to control.

When silence finally fell, only empty robes remained where Ravenna had stood. The rescued hostages wept with relief as Alice freed them. Ethan, still in wolf form, stood guard while Lila closed the Archive with trembling hands.

"It's really over?" Alice asked, approaching her companions.

The massive wolf growled softly, pressing against her side while Lila managed a tired smile. "This battle is. But Daybridge's story isn't finished."

They emerged into the night air, forever changed by their confrontation with ancient hatred and the power of their unity. The Bloodline Archive pulsed gently in Lila's grasp, no longer a tool of vengeance but a symbol of balance restored.

The wolf raised its head and howled - a sound echoed by the Archive's gentle hum and the whisper of Alice's blessed bolts. Three different powers, united in protection of their town, ready for whatever darkness might come next.

"The Archive showed me something," Lila said, spreading ancient pages across the PDU's conference table. "Each town's supernatural defense evolved differently. Trying to standardize them..."

"Would be like trying to standardize ecosystems," Alice finished. "Some things have to grow naturally."

CHAPTER TWENTY-NINE

THE FINAL REVELATION

THUNDER CRACKED above the university's bell tower as Nadia rushed up the spiral staircase, the ancient pendant burning against her skin. Behind her, Alice's voice rang out in Latin, holding back the shadows that pursued them. Ahead, moonlight filtered through the tower's broken windows, illuminating the final battleground.

"They're channeling power from all thirteen sites," Nadia called Alice. "The old witch-marks are activating across Daybridge."

The pendant showed her what mortal eyes couldn't see – ley lines blazing beneath the city streets, forming a twisted version of the protection circle the original Daughters had created. But where their magic had sealed darkness away, this new coven was trying to draw it in.

They burst onto the tower's top level. Ethan was already there, wrestling with something that wore Professor Jones' face but wasn't her anymore. Dark energy crackled around the possessed woman's form.

"The grimoire!" Nadia shouted. "Get the grimoire!"

The book lay open on a makeshift altar, its pages turning by themselves in a wind that smelled of grave dirt and burning roses. The corrupt coven had translated the text wrong – deliberately wrong. They thought they were summoning power. They didn't realize they were being used.

"Little chronicler," Professor Jones' voice distorted, multiple tones speaking at once. "Always watching, never understanding. Your ancestor made the same mistake."

"No," Nadia's fingers clutched Elizabeth's journal. "She understood perfectly. That's why she left us the key."

The pendant flared as she spoke, responding to the power building in the tower. Around them, the thirteen corrupt witch-marks pulsed in sync, trying to complete their dark circle.

"Alice, now!"

Alice raised her hands, silver light flowing from her fingers. The pendant caught it, amplified it, sending it racing along the ley lines. Across Daybridge, the original protective marks that the Daughters had hidden centuries ago began to wake.

"You can't stop what's coming," the thing wearing Jones sneered. "The void remembers. It hungers."

"It lies," Nadia's voice rang with certainty as she pulled Elizabeth's journal from her bag. "I've read the true account. The Caligari Cataclysm wasn't an accident or a natural disaster. It was a prison, created by the Daughters to contain something that never should have been summoned."

She began to read from the journal, her voice joining with Alice's chant. The pendant grew brighter, recognizing the words of its original wielders. Around them, the tower's stones thrummed with awakening power.

"The circle must be complete," the thing in Chen shrieked. "The thirteen must—"

"Look again," Nadia held up the pendant. "Count the marks. The Daughters didn't make thirteen witch-marks. They made fourteen."

Understanding bloomed in Alice's eyes as she grabbed Nadia's free hand. Ethan's fingers closed around her other wrist, completing their circle. The pendant blazed like a captured star.

"The fourteenth mark was hidden in plain sight," Nadia continued, her voice growing stronger as the pendant's power flowed through her. "The university itself. Built on the site of the original binding. That's why you chose this place, isn't it? But you never saw the full pattern."

She pulled out her research notes, letting them fall around the altar. Photographs, maps, and diagrams scattered across the stones, forming a new pattern. The true pattern.

"The fourteen points don't form a summoning circle," she declared. "They form a seal. And we're standing at its heart."

The pendant's light exploded outward as Nadia spoke the final words from Elizabeth's journal. Power surged through the ley lines, but instead of drawing darkness in, it pushed it back. The corrupt witch-marks shattered one by one, replaced by the original Daughters' sigils.

Professor Jones' body convulsed as the darkness was torn from her. Above them, the storm clouds parted, revealing a perfect circle of stars around the moon.

"The seal," Alice breathed. "It's reforming."

"Not just reforming," Nadia watched as the fourteen marks blazed across Daybridge like a constellation fallen to earth. "Growing stronger. The Daughters didn't just seal the darkness away. They created a living ward, powered by the town itself. By its protectors."

She looked at her hands, watching silver light dance across her skin. The pendant's power had changed her, awakened something that had always been there, dormant in her blood.

"Knowledge isn't just power," she said softly, remembering Elizabeth's words. "It's purpose."

As the light faded and the seal settled into place, Nadia felt the weight of generations shift. She was more than just a chronicler now. The pendant's warmth reminded her of her new role – not just to record history, but to guard against its darkest chapters repeating.

Professor Jones groaned, herself again. Ethan moved to help her while Alice began cleansing the altar. But Nadia's eyes were drawn to the town below, where fourteen points of light pulsed steadily, keeping watch.

The price of knowledge had been high, but its reward was greater: understanding at last what her ancestor had tried to tell her. Some secrets weren't meant to be buried. They were meant to be understood, protected, passed down.

She touched the pendant, feeling its power settle into a quiet hum. The darkness would try again – it always did. But now she knew what she was, what her family had always been: not just witnesses to the light, but its guardians.

And Daybridge would endure, as it always had, under the watch of its fourteen stars.

CHAPTER THIRTY

THE ARCHITECT'S DILEMMA

Robert Payne's office occupied the top floor of one of Daybridge's few modern buildings, a glass and steel structure that somehow blended with the colonial architecture surrounding it. Ethan noticed the subtle details as they rode the elevator: the iron inlays in the doorframes, the rowan wood panels, and the barely visible sigils etched into the corner of each window.

"Impressive wards," Alice murmured, her hunter's senses picking up the layered protections.

The elevator opened directly into Payne's office, where floor-to-ceiling windows offered a panoramic view of Daybridge. The architect stood at his drafting table, his silver-streaked hair disheveled, sleeves rolled up to reveal forearms covered in graphite smudges. He was working on what seemed to be renovation plans for the old courthouse, but Ethan's enhanced vision caught the subtle protective symbols hidden within the architectural details.

"Detective Reeves," Payne straightened, running a hand through his hair. "And Miss Chen. I wondered when you'd come asking about the buildings."

He gestured to a seating area where blueprints and material samples covered every surface. Moving a stack of papers, he revealed chairs that Ethan recognized as being made from iron-reinforced oak.

"You've been busy," Ethan observed, noting the dark circles under Payne's eyes.

"Too busy." Payne collapsed into his chair, loosening his tie. "Do you know how many renovations requests I've received in the past month? Everyone wants 'updates' to their homes and businesses. They don't say why, but they all have the same look in their eyes."

He pulled out a drawer, retrieving a bottle of scotch and three glasses. "Fear. They're terrified. And they should be."

Alice picked up one of the blueprints – plans for a new apartment complex. "These protective measures... they're extensive."

"And expensive," Payne poured three fingers of scotch into each glass. "Iron nails hand-forged by traditional methods. Rowan wood imported from Scotland. Silver inlays in the foundation corners. Salt mixed into the concrete at precise ratios. Each building is basically a fortress against the supernatural."

He drained his glass in one go. "The problem is, I can't explain any of this to the planning board or the contractors. Try telling a construction crew why they need to use hand-forged nails that cost ten times more than regular ones. Or why the window frames need to be aligned with the cardinal directions."

"How are you managing it?" Ethan asked.

"Creative accounting. Calling them 'historical preservation require-ments.' Playing up the tourist angle – people love authentic colonial craftsmanship." Payne laughed bitterly. "I'm burning through favors faster than I can replenish them. And it's still not enough."

He stood, moving to the windows. The late afternoon sun cast long shadows across Daybridge's rooftops. "Look out there. Really look. What do you see?"

Ethan joined him, his wolf's eyes picking up details human vision would miss. The town was a patchwork of old and new, protected and vulnerable. Some buildings glowed with the subtle energy of wards, while others stood dark and exposed.

"A town divided," Alice said softly, coming to stand with them.

"Exactly." Payne pressed his palm against the glass. "The old families, the ones who know – they're fortifying their properties. But what about everyone else? The regular people who live here, who have no idea what's really happening? Every time I design a new building without proper protections, I feel like I'm creating a potential deathtrap."

He returned to his desk, pulling out a worn leather journal. "My grandfather was an architect too. He left me this. Instructions for incorporating protective elements into buildings, passed down through generations of Asian master builders. He called it 'defensive architecture.' I always thought it was superstition until..."

"Until the murders started," Ethan finished.

"Until I saw things that shouldn't exist walking down Main Street in broad daylight." Payne opened the journal, revealing intricate diagrams. "The old protections are failing. Whatever's coming... conventional walls won't stop it."

Alice studied the diagrams. "These designs... they're not just physical protection. They're meant to channel and amplify natural ley lines."

"The entire town sits on a network of them." Payne pulled out a map marked with intersecting lines of energy. "The original settlers knew this. They built Daybridge's most important buildings at power nexus points. But modern development has disrupted many of these connections."

He spread out several blueprints, each marked with both architectural details and mystical annotations. "I'm trying to restore those connections, building by building. But it's like trying to repair a spider's web with boxing gloves on. One wrong move, and..."

"The whole pattern falls apart," Alice finished.

Payne nodded wearily. "And then there's the ethical dilemma. Every time I incorporate these protections, I'm essentially choosing who lives and who dies if the worst happens. The people who can afford custom renovations get safety. Everyone else..."

He trailed off, staring at the plans before him. "I've started doing pro bono work for schools and public buildings. Working nights, weekends. My wife thinks I'm having an affair – with architecture." He laughed, but there was no humor in it. "Maybe I am. This has consumed my life."

Ethan picked up a material sample – a piece of iron worked with intricate patterns. "You're doing what you can."

"But is it enough?" Payne's voice cracked slightly. "Last week, I watched Mrs. Henderson's youngest daughter playing in the park. All I could think about was whether the wards I installed in the playground equipment would be strong enough to protect her if... when..."

He straightened suddenly, his professional demeanor returning like a mask. "You're not here just to discuss building codes, Detective. What do you need?"

"Information," Ethan said. "About the buildings where the victims were found. And any properties owned by the old families that might be significant."

Payne nodded, moving to his computer. "I'll give you everything I have. But be careful – in Daybridge, architecture isn't just about buildings anymore. It's about survival."

As he compiled the files, Payne added quietly, "And Detective? If you stop whatever's causing this... tell me. Maybe then I can finally get a full night's sleep without dreaming of iron nails and rowan wood."

The sun had set by the time they left, casting Payne's protective symbols into sharp relief against the darkening sky. From his office window, the architect watched them go, then turned back to his drafting table. There were more buildings to fortify, more lives to protect, and the darkness wasn't waiting for anyone to be ready.

EPILOGUE: THE NEXT CHAPTER

The Classroom Lesson

Ms. Maddy Lawson's eighth-grade history class occupied one of Daybridge Middle School's oldest rooms. Ethan noticed the fresh iron fixtures on the windows and the salt lines discretely embedded in the newly installed baseboards as he and Alice slipped into seats at the back of the classroom. The renovations had been Payne's work – protection disguised as historical restoration.

"Can anyone tell me why Daybridge was founded in this particular location?" Ms. Lawson asked, her chalk tapping against a map that showed the town as it existed in 1682. She was young for a teacher, barely thirty, with dark skin and elaborate braids tied back with what Ethan recognized as protective threads.

A girl in the front row – Emma Payne, the architect's daughter – raised her hand. "Because of the confluence of rivers?"

"That's the answer in your textbook," Ms. Lawson smiled. "But what else? Think about the stories your grandparents tell."

The class shifted uncomfortably. After recent events, those old family stories carried new weight.

A boy near the window spoke up hesitantly. "My grandmother says it's because of the lines."

"Lines?" Ms. Lawson's chalk traced invisible patterns on the map.

"The... energy lines?" He glanced around nervously. "She says they're like rivers, but for magic."

Instead of dismissing the answer, Ms. Lawson nodded. "Ley lines. The original settlers chose this location because it sits at a crossroads of natural energy. They believed these lines could offer both power and protection."

Ethan watched the students' reactions. Some nodded knowingly – children of the old families. Others looked skeptical, but there was an undercurrent of uncertainty. They'd all seen too much lately to dismiss such things.

"The founders built the town's most important buildings at specific points." Ms. Lawson drew circles on the map. "The town hall. The church. The library. Can anyone guess why?"

Emma Payne raised her hand again. "To create a pattern? Like the symbols my dad draws on his blueprints when he thinks no one's looking?"

A ripple of recognition went through the class. Many had seen similar marks appearing around town during the recent renovations.

"Exactly." Ms. Lawson put down her chalk. "Daybridge was designed as more than just a town. It was built to be a sanctuary – a place where different kinds of people could live together safely."

"Different kinds?" A student in the back asked.

Ms. Lawson's eyes met Ethan's briefly. "People with different beliefs, different backgrounds, different... abilities. The founders understood that diversity made the town stronger, not weaker."

She pulled down another map, this one showing modern Daybridge. "But somewhere along the way, we started forgetting. We paved over the old protections. Built new buildings without considering the patterns. Dismissed the old stories as superstition."

"Until now," Emma said quietly.

The class fell silent. Everyone knew about the murders, the strange sightings, the way their parents whispered behind closed doors.

"Until now," Ms. Lawson agreed. "But here's something important to remember: Daybridge has faced challenges before. The witch trials. The Dark Summer of 1892. The Shadows of 1963. Each time, the town survived because people came together. They remembered the old wisdom while finding new solutions."

She walked between the desks, making eye contact with each student. "That's why understanding our history is so important. Not just the sanitized version in your textbooks, but the real history. The stories your grandparents tell. The symbols in the architecture. The traditions that might seem odd but serve a purpose."

A girl with bright red hair raised her hand. "Is that why they're putting iron in all the buildings? My mom says it's for historical accuracy, but..."

"Iron has many properties," Ms. Lawson said carefully. "Throughout history, people have used it for both construction and protection. The founders understood this dual purpose."

"Like the salt in the new sidewalks?" another student asked. "And the weird trees they're planting in the park?"

"Rowan trees," Emma supplied. "My dad says they're traditional."

Ms. Lawson smiled. "You're all noticing things. Good. Observation is the first step toward understanding. Daybridge is changing, adapting. Just like it has before."

She returned to the front of the room, picking up a piece of chalk that Ethan now realized was made of compressed herbs and blessed materials. "Your assignment for next week: Interview an older family member about Daybridge's history. Ask about the stories they were told as children. Pay attention to the details that might seem strange or magical."

The bell rang, but before the students could leave, Ms. Lawson added, "And remember – every town has its secrets. Daybridge just happens to be more honest about them these days."

As the students filed out, several paused to study the protection symbols newly carved into the doorframe. Emma Ming lingered, looking at Ethan and Alice with knowing eyes before following her classmates.

Ms. Lawson approached them once the room was empty. "Detective Reeves. Miss Chen. I assume you're here about the new curriculum?"

"The school board approved teaching this?" Alice asked, gesturing to the maps with their marked ley lines.

"They approved a 'comprehensive local history program," Ms. Lawson smiled. "What that means is... open to interpretation. These kids aren't blind. They see what's happening in town. Better they learn about it properly than piece it together from rumors and fear."

Ethan studied the young teacher. "You're from one of the old families."

"Third generation teacher, eighth generation... practitioner." She adjusted a crystal pendant at her neck. "Education has always been our way of protecting the next generation. Knowledge is power, especially in Daybridge."

She began erasing the chalkboard, though Ethan noticed she left the ley line markings. "The children need to understand their heritage – all of it. The good and the bad. The normal and the supernatural. It's the only way they'll be prepared for whatever comes next."

"And their parents?" Alice asked.

"Are starting to remember their own lessons." Ms. Lawson smiled. "It's amazing how quickly people recall the old ways when they need them. Fear can be a powerful teacher, but hope is a better one."

She gathered her materials, including a leather-bound book that hummed with subtle energy. "If you'll excuse me, I have a faculty meeting. We're discussing how to incorporate protective techniques into physical education without alarming the superintendent."

At the door, she paused. "Detective Reeves? Thank you. For everything you did last week. The children might not know the details, but they know something has changed. They feel safer."

After she left, Ethan and Alice stood in the empty classroom, surrounded by maps showing a town's evolution and chalk marks revealing its true nature.

"Think it will work?" Alice asked. "Teaching them like this?"

Ethan watched through the window as students crossed the playground, unconsciously avoiding the areas where the new wards were strongest. "They're already learning. The question is, what will they do with that knowledge?"

A bell rang, and somewhere in the building, another class began learning about Daybridge's unique place in the world – one careful lesson at a time.

The Archivist's Legacy

One Month Later

Nadia's study had transformed, much like its owner. Gone were the chaotic piles of research and frantic notes. Instead, carefully cataloged journals lined the walls, each containing verified accounts of Daybridge's supernatural history. The pendant rested in a crafted silver holder on her desk, its subtle glow reflecting off the crystals Alice had helped her arrange around the room.

She stood before her evidence wall, which now displayed a proper map of Daybridge's fourteen ward points. Red strings had been replaced with silver threads that pulsed faintly with protective magic. Each connection represented a story she had finally pieced together.

"The latest from the Council," Alice said, entering with a stack of letters. "They're still processing everything that happened at the foundry."

Nadia smiled, touching the small streak of silver that now marked her dark hair – a permanent reminder of the power that had flowed through her that night. "Let me guess: more questions about the four-teenth ward?"

"Among other things." Alice settled into what had become her usual chair. "They're calling you the Archivist now, you know. Officially."

"Elizabeth would have liked that." Nadia picked up her great-great-grandmother's journal, its pages now translated and understood. "Though I think she always knew this was coming. Listen to this entry from 1893:

"The true power of our legacy lies not in the keeping of secrets, but in knowing when to reveal them. Each generation of Marsh women has served as a bridge – between past and present, between knowledge and action, between darkness and light. We are not mere chroniclers. We are guardians of truth, keepers of balance."

She placed the journal carefully on its stand. Beside it sat her own jour-nal, its pages filling with new observations and insights. The pendant's power had awakened something in her blood, sharpening her percep-tions. She saw Daybridge differently now – the way magic flowed through its streets, the subtle barriers between worlds, the marks left by centuries of supernatural activity.

"Professor Jones came by earlier," Alice mentioned. "The university board approved your proposal."

Nadia nodded, gesturing to the plans on her desk. The Daybridge Historical Archive would have a new wing, dedicated to what she now called "alternative historical studies." A safe place to preserve the true records of their town's supernatural heritage.

"It's not just about storing information anymore," she explained, pulling up blueprints on her computer. "We need to prepare the next generation. There are other families like mine out there – descendants of the original guardians who don't know their heritage."

Her phone chimed with a text from Ethan: "Activity at site Seven. Nothing serious. But you might want to document this one."

"Speaking of which," Alice raised an eyebrow. "Your first official student is here."

A young woman entered hesitantly – Toni Jones, the professor's daughter. She carried a journal of her own, filled with questions about her family's connection to Daybridge's magical history.

"Ms. Marsh," Toni began. "I want to understand... everything."

Nadia touched the pendant, feeling its warm response to Toni's presence. Another bloodline awakening, another piece of the pattern revealing itself.

"Understanding comes with responsibility," she said, echoing Elizabeth's words. "Are you ready for that?"

Toni's eyes fell on the silver streak in Nadia's hair, then to the ward map with its glowing connections. "Yes. I need to know what my mother was involved in, what's really happening in this town."

"Then let's start at the beginning." Nadia pulled out a chair and opened her journal. "Daybridge was founded in 1789, but its true history begins much earlier. There were fourteen families chosen to protect something ancient, something powerful..."

As she spoke, the pendant's light strengthened slightly, recognizing the passing of knowledge from one guardian to another. Outside, a soft rain began to fall, carrying whispers of magic through Daybridge's streets. The fourteen wards pulsed in harmony, maintaining their ancient vigil.

Nadia felt the weight of her role settle more comfortably on her shoulders. She had found her place in the pattern – preserving history and shaping its course. The darkness would return, as it always did, wearing new faces and bringing new challenges.

But she would be ready. They would all be ready.

In her mind, she could almost hear Elizabeth's approval as she began teaching Toni the first lessons of their shared legacy. This was what it meant to be the Archivist – a keeper of secrets and a guide for people who would carry them forward.

The silver in her hair caught the light as she turned a page, beginning another chapter in Daybridge's endless story. Some prices were worth paying, some burdens worth bearing, if it meant protecting what mattered most.

Knowledge. Truth. Home.

The sun rose over the city of Daybridge, casting a warm glow across the streets and buildings. It had been three months since the defeat of the Witch Queen, and slowly but surely, the city was healing. The scars of the past were still there, visible in the haunted eyes of the survivors and the ruined buildings that dotted the landscape, but there was also a sense of hope, a feeling that the worst was behind them and that a new day was dawning.

For Ethan Reeves and Alice Chen, life had taken on a new sense of purpose. They had always been dedicated to their work as detectives, but now, they knew that their role went far beyond solving crimes and catching criminals. They were the guardians of Daybridge, the protectors of the innocent against the forces of darkness that threatened to destroy everything they held dear.

As they walked through the streets of the city, their eyes scanning the shadows for any sign of trouble, they couldn't help but feel a sense of pride. They had faced the Witch Queen and her minions, had fought against impossible odds and emerged victorious. But they also knew that their work was far from over.

The events of the ghost witch uprising had sent shockwaves through the supernatural community, and they knew that it was only a matter of time before new threats emerged. There were whispers of dark forces gathering in the shadows, of ancient evils stirring from their slumber, and Ethan and Alice knew that they would have to be ready to face whatever challenges lay ahead.

But they also knew that they were not alone. The people of Daybridge had seen the truth of the supernatural world, had seen the horrors that lurked in the shadows, and they knew that they could no longer ignore the darkness that threatened to engulf them.

Everywhere they went, Ethan and Alice saw signs of a city coming together, of people banding together to rebuild and protect their home. Neighborhood watch groups formed, patrolling the streets and keeping an eye out for any sign of trouble. Community centers opened their doors, offering shelter and support to those who had lost everything in the uprising.

And in the heart of the city, a new force was rising. The Daybridge Paranormal Defense Unit, a team of experts and specialists dedicated to investigating and combating supernatural threats. Ethan and Alice had been invited to join the unit, to lend their skills and expertise to the fight against the forces of darkness.

It was a daunting task, but one they knew they could not refuse. The people of Daybridge needed them, needed the protection and guidance that only they could provide. And so, with heavy hearts and determined spirits, they had accepted the invitation, knowing that their lives would never be the same.

As they made their way through the city streets, their minds racing with thoughts of the future, they couldn't help but feel a sense of excitement. The world was changing, and they were at the forefront of that change. They had the power to make a difference, to shape the future of Daybridge and the world beyond.

But even as they looked to the future, they couldn't help but feel a sense of unease. Lila was still out there somewhere, her motives and allegiances still unclear. And the Witch Queen's final message still echoed in their minds, a chilling reminder that the war was far from over.

They knew that they would have to be vigilant, always on their guard against the forces of darkness that threatened to destroy everything they held dear. But they also knew that they had each other, and the strength and courage to face whatever challenges lay ahead.

As they reached the steps of the Daybridge Paranormal Defense Unit headquarters, Ethan and Alice paused for a moment, their eyes meeting in a silent moment of understanding. They had been through so much together, had faced the darkest of evils and emerged stronger for it.

And now, as they stepped through the doors and into the unknown, they knew that they were ready for whatever lay ahead. The next chapter of their lives was beginning, and they would face it head-on, with the strength and determination that had brought them this far.

Ethan and Alice stood side by side, ready to face whatever challenges the world may throw their way, secure knowing that they had each other and the support of the people of Daybridge.

And as the sun sets over the city, casting long shadows across the streets and buildings, there is a sense that the darkness has been pushed back, that the light has won out against the forces of evil. The ghost witches may be gone, but the fight against the supernatural is far from over. And Ethan and Alice will be there, ready to stand against the darkness, no matter what form it may take.

A SNEAK PEEK AT WHAT'S NEXT!

Thank you for joining me on this journey through *Shadows of Vengeance.* I hope you enjoyed exploring the mysteries of Daybridge and getting to know its secrets.

The story doesn't end here—there's so much more waiting to be uncovered. I'm excited to give you an exclusive first look at **Moonlight Origins: The Making of a Werewolf Detective**, the next book in the *Ethan Reeves Werewolf Detective Series*. Dive into the free chapter below and get a taste of what's to come!

Moonlight Origins: The Making of a Werewolf Detective - Book Four in the Ethan Reeves Werewolf Detective Series

Prologue: Night of the First Change

The full moon hung like a spotlight in the October sky as Detective Ethan Reeves chased the suspect down Harper Street. His lungs burned, but something else burned deeper - an unfamiliar fire in his blood that had been building all day. Sweat drenched his shirt despite the autumn chill.

"Police! Stop!" His voice came out as more growl than command, startling even him.

The suspect darted into Oakwood Cemetery, weaving between weathered headstones. Ethan followed, but his vision kept blurring, shifting between crystal clarity and strange colors he'd never seen before. The world seemed to pulse with new smells - wet earth, rotting leaves, old stone, and something metallic that made his stomach turn.

His bones ached like they were trying to reshape themselves. This wasn't normal exhaustion. This was something else, something that traced back to that bizarre attack three weeks ago. The doctors had found no infection, said the wounds healed unusually fast. Too fast.

The suspect scaled the cemetery's back wall. Ethan moved to follow, but a shaft of moonlight hit him directly. The burning erupted into white-hot agony. He dropped to his knees, watching in horror as his fingers began to elongate.

His jaw cracked and extended, teeth sharpening into points as fur erupted across his skin. The pain was excruciating, but worse was the hunger - a primal, ravening thing clawing its way up from deep inside. His senses exploded with information: the rapid heartbeat of a rabbit hiding in the bushes fifty yards away, the lingering scent of cigarette smoke from a groundskeeper's break hours ago, the whisper of cars on the highway two miles distant.

Through the haze of transformation, he saw movement at the top of the cemetery wall. The suspect - no, not suspect, he realized as his enhanced vision cut through the darkness. Hunter. The figure perched there watching him, lips curled in a predatory smile that revealed gleaming fangs.

"Welcome to the pack, Detective Reeves," the hunter said, voice carrying easily to Ethan's newly sensitive ears. "We've been waiting for you."

Then the hunter was gone, leaving Ethan alone with the moon, the night, and the terrifying knowledge that everything he thought he knew about his city's dark underbelly was just the surface of a much deeper, more dangerous reality.

His police radio crackled with his partner's voice, searching for him. But he couldn't answer anymore. Not like this. Not ever again as just a normal detective.

The change took him completely then, and Detective Ethan Reeves vanished into the shadows of Oakwood Cemetery, replaced by something that howled at the moon and ran with four legs instead of two.

The hunt was on, but he wasn't sure anymore who was the hunter and who was the prey.

~

ABOUT THE AUTHOR

Rae Stonehouse turned to fiction writing after establishing himself as a prolific author of self-development and professional growth books.

With over 50 published works helping readers navigate personal and professional challenges, he embarked on a new creative path with the Ethan Reeves Werewolf Detective Series.

When not weaving tales of supernatural sleuthing, Stonehouse continues to share his expertise in personal development through workshops and speaking engagements from his home in British Columbia.

The Ethan Reeves series marks his debut in fiction writing, blending his understanding of human nature with a newfound passion for urban fantasy.